THE
ODYSSEY

THE ODYSSEY

RETOLD BY Gillian Cross

ILLUSTRATED BY Neil Packer

CANDLEWICK PRESS

For Martin, with lots of love

Gillian

For Emily Carol Bickerton [1965–2008]
Love, Neil and Arvo

CONTENTS

O
ut of the mysterious past comes this tale of human endurance, full of unknown dangers and terrifying monsters. It tells the adventures of a man who spent ten years fighting the anger of the raging sea as he struggled to sail home.

This is the story of Odysseus of Ithaca, cleverest of all the kings of ancient Greece.

THE WAR

IIIIIIIIIIIIIIIIIIIIIIIIIIIIIIIIIIIIIIIIIIIII

IT WAS WAR THAT forced Odysseus to leave his home. When Paris of Troy ran off with the king of Sparta's wife, her husband gathered an army to fetch her back. And he called on all his fellow kings to join him — including Odysseus.

There was no escape. Odysseus wanted to stay on Ithaca with his own wife, Penelope, and their baby son, Telemachus. But the other kings needed his quick wits and his cunning. When he didn't come, they went to Ithaca to find him.

"Sparta is your ally," they said. "You swore to fight side by side with the Spartans. And that means helping to fetch Helen back from Troy."

It was true. All the Greek kings had promised to help one another. With a heavy heart, Odysseus called his soldiers together and prepared a fleet of ships.

The night before they left, he talked to Penelope, his wife. "This will be a fierce and bitter war," he said. "If I die, you are in charge of Ithaca. But only while Telemachus grows up. When he's a man, he'll take over, and you must get out of his way. Choose another husband for yourself and go to live with him."

"I don't want any husband except you," Penelope said with tears in her eyes.

"That's how it must be," Odysseus insisted. "Promise to do what I ask."

Still with tears in her eyes, Penelope promised. "But you *will* come back," she said fiercely. "I know you will."

"That depends on the gods," Odysseus said. He kissed her good-bye and hugged Telemachus.

Then he went down to the long ships in the harbor, and he and his men set sail over the wine-dark sea.

For nine long, bloodstained years, the Greek army besieged the golden city of Troy, battering at its walls in vain, while the gods watched from their home on high Olympus.

For nine lonely years, Penelope stayed in Ithaca, taking care of the kingdom and waiting for the war to finish. As Telemachus grew tall and strong, she told him about his father, Odysseus, the cleverest king in Greece.

"When the war ends," she said, "he will come back to us."

In the tenth year of fighting, the Greeks tricked their way into Troy. The war ended in a storm of blood and fire, and the golden city of Troy was burned to ruins. One by one, the kings of Greece trailed home across the sea.

Except Odysseus.

Where was he?

No one knew, except the gods, gazing down from high Olympus: Zeus, the father of gods and men; Athene the goddess of wisdom; Hermes, the giant killer and messenger of the gods; and Poseidon, the dark earth-shaker god who controlled the ocean. Only they saw the whole, long story as it unfolded.

TRAVELING INTO DISASTER

ODYSSEUS LEFT TROY with twelve ships full of weary, homesick men. The wind was in their favor, but they weren't carrying enough food and water for the journey.

When they came to the city of the Cicones, they went ashore, killing all the men and taking what they needed. It was a stupid, greedy attack, and the sailors made it worse. When Odysseus ordered them back to their ships, they refused to obey him. They'd just finished fighting a long, fierce war, and they wanted to rest and feast.

Ignoring Odysseus, they butchered the sheep and cattle they'd captured and barbecued them on the beach. As they worked, they broke open barrels of wine and started drinking steadily.

By the time night came, they were all incapable. They slumped down onto the sand and fell asleep beside their dying fires.

It was disastrously stupid.

While they slept, the Cicones were creeping around in the hills, gathering reinforcements. At dawn, a wild army came sweeping down from the hills, looking for revenge.

Odysseus's men were woken by the clash of spears and the rattle of chariot wheels. Leaping up in a panic, they snatched at their weapons, but it was too late to form a battle line. They had to defend themselves as best they could, fighting hand to hand all over the beach.

They held out until evening. Then the Cicones overwhelmed them, slaughtering more than seventy men. The others ran for their ships, exhausted and terrified.

They scrambled aboard frantically, hoisting the sails and hauling on their oars. It was impossible to recover the bodies of their comrades. All they could do was call out a sad good-bye as they left them behind on the beach.

And there was no chance to rest once they were out at sea. As soon as the land disappeared, a great storm hit them, blackening the sky and ripping their sails to pieces. Raging winds blew them off course, driving them out, past Cythera into the River of Ocean beyond.

For nine days, the storm howled around them without stopping. There was nowhere to land. Dense cloud hid the sun in the daytime and the stars at night, and even Odysseus couldn't figure out where they were.

19

On the tenth day, the wind dropped suddenly and the sky cleared. They found themselves sailing beside a strange and beautiful shore covered in thick vegetation. It looked completely uninhabited.

"Drop anchor here!" Odysseus called across the water.

The twelve ships anchored side by side, and the sailors lowered little boats to take them ashore. This time they were much more cautious. Odysseus looked around warily as they landed, and they were all watching out for enemies. But nothing moved except the leaves rustling in the breeze.

By now, they were desperately short of food and water, but this time Odysseus didn't send them all inland. He kept most of the men down on the beach to guard the boats. Only three of them were picked to go off and explore.

He warned them to be careful. "If you meet any people, treat them politely," he said. "Tell them that this is a peaceful visit — that all we want is food and water." The three men headed off down a winding path that led into the trees.

The others were left behind to keep watch, and they settled down beside the boats, alert for any sign of danger. All they could do was wait.

And wait. And wait . . .

The sun rose high in the sky, driving them almost mad with thirst, but Odysseus wouldn't let them leave the beach. They had to endure the full heat of the day, and they were still there at sunset, when the light began to grow dim.

Where were the three men who had gone exploring?

Odysseus was anxious not to spend the night on the beach. That was too dangerous. But he couldn't abandon the men he had sent inland. What had happened to them? Were they dead?

He had to know.

Dividing the rest of the sailors into two groups, he left one group with the boats. Then he led the other group along the path the three explorers had taken. It was very dark now, and they peered nervously into the undergrowth as they went, but nothing moved except their own shadows.

In less than ten minutes, they came to a clearing surrounded by tall trees tangled with vines.

The vines were dripping with clusters of golden fruit that brushed against their heads as they passed. The air was heavy with its rich, honeyed scent.

Ahead of them, all across the clearing, people were lounging on the grass. Men, women, and children sprawled together, languidly sucking at the golden fruit. And in the very center of the group, their hands full of fruit and their faces distant and entranced, were the three lost men Odysseus had come to find.

"What are you doing?" he shouted at them. "Why are you idling here while the rest of us are waiting on the beach? We need to take on food and water and set sail for Ithaca."

The three men looked up with stupid, vacant smiles.

"Why should we struggle on?" one of them murmured. "What is Ithaca? Only a barren rock in the wide sea."

"It's where your wives and families live," Odysseus said fiercely.

The empty smiles didn't change.

"What do wives and families matter?" said another of the men. "Nothing compares to being here, eating the lotus fruit."

The lotus eaters beside him held out handfuls of fruit, calling to Odysseus and his companions.

"Come here and lie with us to eat the lotus. The sea is cold and cruel, and the lands beyond have no delights like this. Forget your homes and families. Stay here. Eat, and forget."

Odysseus saw the man next to him take a step forward into the clearing. Some of the others were wavering, staring at the lotus fruit. Unless he acted quickly, they would give in to their curiosity and taste it. Then he would lose them all.

He lowered his voice and began whispering orders quickly.

"We have to get our comrades back to the ship. Rush in and carry them off, without listening to what they say. And *don't taste the fruit*. Don't even lick the juice from your fingers. This is a terrible place."

His sailors obeyed, charging forward to seize their companions. Drugged by the honey-scented lotus, the three on the ground were taken by surprise. As they were hoisted up, they dropped the fruit they were holding. Immediately, they began to wail and scream.

"Give us back the lotus!"

"How can we live without it?"

"Put us down! This is the only home we need. Leave us here!"

Their cries were useless. Odysseus had them carried down to the boats and tied up tightly, to stop them from rushing straight back to the lotus eaters. He had no intention of setting them free until the effect of the fruit had worn off. They were taken on board and pushed under the benches, out of the way of the oars.

Then the boats headed back to where the ships were anchored. They had failed to take on any extra food or fresh water, but Odysseus dared not stay any longer. If the rest of his men decided to taste the lotus fruit, none of them would ever reach home.

So they left the beautiful, treacherous land of the lotus eaters and headed out again into the open sea.

As night fell, a thick fog came down over the sea. Within half an hour, the ships were moving in total darkness. There were no stars to guide them. There was no light from the moon.

They didn't realize that they were near land — until they heard the unmistakable scraping noise of their ships running aground.

Hastily lowering their sails, they dropped anchor and jumped into the water. Through the fog, a dark mass of land loomed ahead of them, but they were too exhausted to think of exploring it. They had just enough energy to stagger up the beach, out of range of the tide. As soon as they felt dry sand under their feet, they lay down and fell asleep, wrapped in their cloaks. They didn't even wonder what kind of land they had found.

T H E GIANT IN THE CAVE

THEY AWOKE TO A BEAUTIFUL, clear dawn — and a fine view. Their ships had run aground in a natural harbor, safely away from the wild, open sea. Behind the harbor was a stretch of rich grassland, with luxuriant woods beyond.

The place seemed to have everything they needed. Huge bunches of grapes grew on wild vines, and a spring of fresh water ran down into the harbor. Looking up at the wooded hills, Odysseus saw a herd of wild goats leaping from rock to rock.

"The gods must have brought us here," he said. He and his men took their bows and spears and went off to hunt the goats. In a very short time they had enough meat to last for days — and they'd discovered that the island was uninhabited. At last it was safe to rest and relax.

They feasted on roasted meat, washed down with wine they'd looted from the Cicones. Afterward, they lay on the beach, gazing across to the mainland. They heard the sound of voices drifting over the water, and the bleating of sheep and goats.

And they saw smoke rising into the evening sky, from fires like theirs.

Idly, as the sun went down, they wondered what kind of people lived over there. They peered across at the dark shore, but no human figures were visible. And, however hard they tried, they couldn't make out what the voices were saying.

Still listening, the sailors fell asleep, one by one, beside the embers of their fires. Only Odysseus stayed awake, looking across the water. As the sky grew black and the stars came out, he stared at the glimmering light of the distant fires.

What was over there? Whose voices could they hear?

As soon as the sun rose, Odysseus was on his feet, giving orders to his men as they awoke.

"Eleven ships must stay here, to take on food and fresh water," he said. "But I'll take my own ship over to the mainland to see what sort of people live there."

He signaled to his crew, and they followed him into the water. Clambering on board their ship, they took up their oars. It wasn't worth raising the sail, so they rowed the short distance to the opposite shore.

Because they were rowing, they were facing backward. It was only when they turned the ship, ready to anchor, that they had their first close look at the place where they were going to land.

It was a strange, unsettling sight. A little way back from the shore, they saw the entrance to a vast cave, shadowed by laurel bushes. In front of the cave was a huge sheep pen, made of great blocks of rough-cut stone. Every block was taller than a man.

What kind of creature could build like that? The sailors glanced nervously at one another, and someone muttered that they ought to row straight back to the island. But Odysseus was curious. He bit his lip thoughtfully, making a plan.

"Most of you must stay and guard the ship," he said. "I'll take twelve men with me to explore the cave."

He chose twelve of the best and bravest, and ordered them to pack up some food. Then he filled a big wineskin with rich, strong wine and jumped into the water to wade ashore.

He and his twelve companions crept up the beach toward the towering sheep pen. Peering through a crack in the wall, they saw that it was full of lambs, but there were no adult sheep. Odysseus guessed that the main flock was up in the high pastures, with their shepherd, whoever he was.

Whatever he was.

That gave them a chance to explore the cave. Odysseus crept cautiously up to the entrance, beckoning his men to follow.

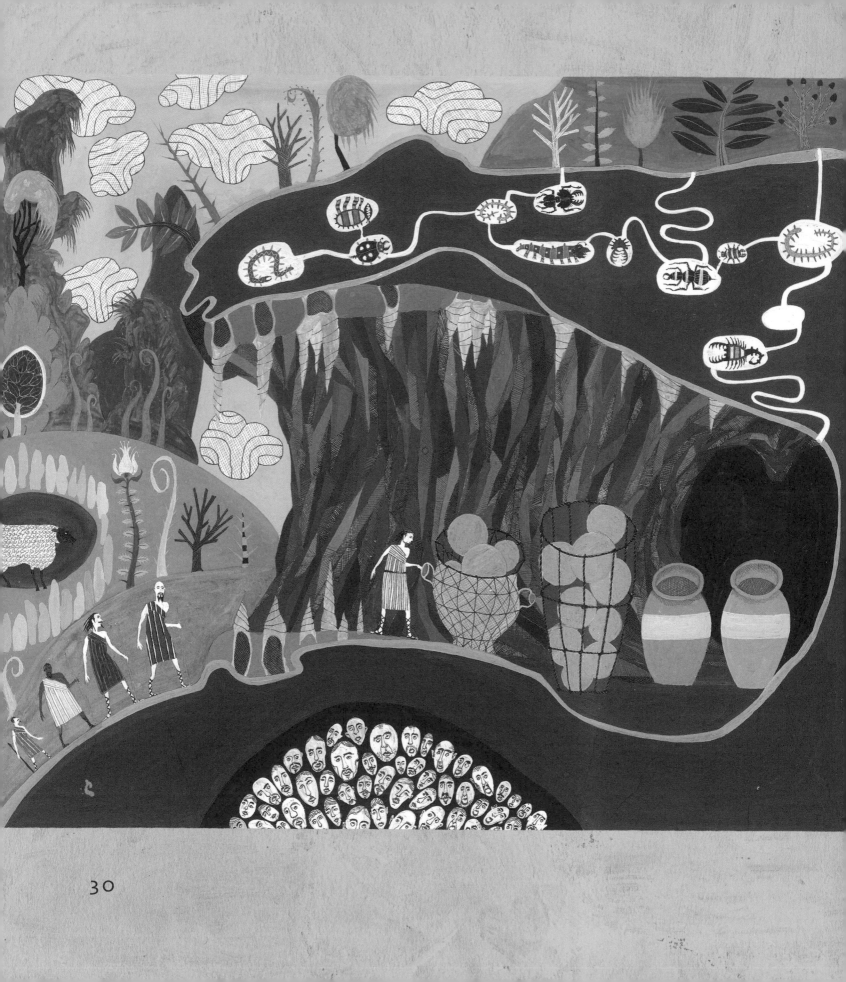

When their eyes adjusted to the darkness inside, they saw an amazing sight.

The cave was very high and deep, and it was full of gigantic baskets and bowls. The baskets were filled with cheeses the size of cart wheels, and the bowls were brimming with milk and whey.

"Look at all this food!" cried one of the sailors. "There are enough cheeses and lambs to last us all the way back to Ithaca."

"We don't need to come as looters," Odysseus said. "I've brought gifts for the owner of this cave. He'll give us gifts in return, out of politeness, and then we'll have all the meat and cheese we need. And we'll have made a new friend, not an enemy."

His men were still nervous, but he persuaded them to stay. Taking dry wood from a stack at the back of the cave, they built themselves a fire and settled down to wait for the owner to return.

They heard him before they saw him.

THUD. THUD. THUD. His footsteps shook the ground ahead of him. In three strides, he had reached the cave and he was driving his sheep inside. A huge bundle of firewood flew in after them — and then came the giant himself. His massive body blocked out the light as he stooped to walk through the entrance.

When Odysseus and his men saw that vast, dark shape, they rushed to the back of the cave to hide in the shadows. By the time they turned around to take another look, the monster was blocking the entrance of the cave with a great slab of stone.

They were trapped.

Shivering in their corner, they watched him sniff at the dying embers of their fire. His massive head turned left and right, peering around. Then he heaped more wood onto the fire.

The flames shot up, and they saw his face for the first time. It was broad and ugly, with a jutting nose and a thick, heavy jaw. In the center of his forehead was a single, hideous eye. His only one.

They were trapped in the cave of a Cyclops.

The monster milked his sheep, guzzling down the first bucketful in a single gulp. He set the rest of the milk aside to curdle for making cheese, and then he built up the fire again, piling the wood so high that the red glare lit up the cave.

This time, he looked around more carefully, searching for intruders. When he saw Odysseus and his men, he bellowed, "Sheep stealers!"

"We're not thieves!" Odysseus said, stepping forward boldly. "We're Greek soldiers, sailing home from the war in Troy."

The Cyclops peered suspiciously at him. "Sailing? Where's your ship, then?"

Odysseus certainly wasn't going to tell him that. He made a sad face and gazed up at the giant.

"Our ship was wrecked," he said. "Poseidon, the earth shaker, whipped up a great storm and swamped it, and we are the only men who didn't drown. Please give us food and shelter."

The Cyclops laughed scornfully. Instead of answering, he reached out and grabbed two of Odysseus's men. Cramming them into his mouth, he gulped them down, grinning as the other sailors shouted in horror.

Then he guzzled another bucketful of milk and sprawled on the floor, falling asleep immediately. His body was like a mountain, filling half the cave.

As soon as he began to snore, Odysseus darted forward, ready to draw his sword. *I can climb up his arm*, he thought, *and stab him while he's asleep.* The sword was halfway out of its scabbard before he realized how stupid he would be to use it.

If he killed the Cyclops, who would let them out of the cave?

He and all his men, working together, would never be able to move the stone that blocked the entrance. Only the Cyclops was strong enough for that. Without him, they would be trapped in the cave forever, doomed to a slow death by starvation.

They had to escape. If they didn't, the Cyclops would eat them all. But they couldn't get out of the cave without his help.

How could they trick him into doing that?

All night, Odysseus lay awake and thought, working out one plan after another. By morning, he knew what he was going to do. But it wouldn't be easy.

The Cyclops had no intention of setting them free. When he awoke, he snatched two more of the men and ate them for his breakfast. Then he rolled the stone away and drove his sheep out of the cave. But he kept a constant watch on Odysseus and his companions to stop them from sneaking out with the sheep. As soon as the whole flock was outside, he followed, grinning cruelly as he pushed the stone back into place.

Odysseus waited until the thunderous footsteps had died away in the distance. Then he took a long pole that was leaning against the wall of the cave.

"This is the weapon we're going to use to defeat the Cyclops," he said.

As he explained the plan to his companions, he used his sword to cut a long piece off the pole. He sharpened it to a point and held the sharpened end in the fire to harden it. Then he hid the finished weapon at the back of the cave — ready for when the Cyclops returned.

It was evening before they heard his terrible feet coming back. *THUD. THUD. THUD.* The stone was dragged away from the mouth of the cave, and in came the sheep. The Cyclops lumbered after them, pulling the stone into place behind him.

The evening went the same way as the one before. The Cyclops milked his sheep and swilled down two bucketfuls of milk. Then he grabbed two sailors for his supper, crunching their bones as he chewed them up. It was a horrific sight, but Odysseus and the rest of his companions forced themselves to stay quiet.

Soon they would have their revenge.

When the Cyclops had finished eating, he settled himself down beside the fire. That was the moment Odysseus had been waiting for. Filling a drinking bowl with the strong wine he'd brought from the ship, he stepped forward, and held it up to the Cyclops.

"I brought this as a gift," he said, "hoping for your help. But I can see that you're too wild and savage to appreciate good wine."

The Cyclops snatched the bowl out of his hand and drank the wine in a single gulp. Then he rolled his single, glaring eye and held out the bowl. "More," he growled. "And when you've poured it, tell me your name. I have a gift for you, too."

Odysseus nodded and smiled, but he didn't speak. Not yet. He just filled the bowl again. And then again after that. And again.

The Cyclops went on guzzling the wine, not realizing how strong it was. Gradually his speech slurred and his eye glazed over. When he was totally drunk, Odysseus spoke at last.

"You asked for my name," he said. "I'll tell you. I'm called Noe Boddy. Now where's the gift you promised me?"

The Cyclops rolled his eye and bellowed with laughter.

"Here it is. *I promise to eat all your

companions before I eat you.* Isn't that a fine gift?

I'll save you until last." He roared with laughter

again and then slumped over onto his back.

In less than a minute, he was snoring drunkenly.

As soon as he was unconscious, Odysseus ran to

the back of cave to fetch the pole he had sharpened.

Once again, he and his men plunged it into the fire.

But this time they held it there until it was red-hot.

When it was just about to burst into flames, they

lifted it out and raised it high in the air.

Then they drove it, with all their strength, into

the Cyclops's one, enormous eye.

He awoke with a scream, knocking them out of the way as he jumped to his feet. And he went on screaming as he struggled to pull the stake out of his eye. The noise awoke every other Cyclops on the hillside, and they all came racing down from their homes, shaking the ground like an earthquake.

"What's the matter, Polyphemus?" they yelled. "Why are you shouting like that? Who's in the cave with you?"

"Noe Boddy!" Polyphemus shouted. "Noe Boddy's here!"

The other giants were baffled. "Has someone hurt you?" they yelled. "Do you want revenge?"

"Noe Boddy has hurt me!" Polyphemus bellowed. "I want revenge on Noe Boddy!"

"Then why are you making such a fuss?" the others shouted angrily. "Be quiet, and let us get to sleep." They stomped away up the hill, leaving Polyphemus blundering around the cave in agony.

The worse the pain grew, the more he wanted revenge. When morning came, he rolled the stone away from the mouth of the cave to let the sheep go out to pasture. But he was determined not to let his enemies escape. Sitting down in the entrance, he stretched out his great arms, running them over the ground to make sure that only sheep got past him.

The sailors looked desperately at one another. What could they do now? If they tried to sneak out with the sheep, they were sure to be caught.

But Odysseus had thought of that — and made another plan. While it was still dark, he'd tied the Cyclops's great sheep together in threes, knotting willow twigs into their thick, curly wool. Now, without making a sound, he showed his men in sign language how to cling on underneath the middle sheep. Once they were up, he tied them securely into place.

As soon as he let the sheep go, they trotted toward the mouth of the cave. Polyphemus ran his hands over their backs and around their feet, searching for the sailors. But the men were hidden in the thick wool and protected by sheep on each side, and he didn't find them.

One by one, they were carried out of the cave, until only Odysseus was left. All the sheep had gone now, except the big ram that led the flock. Jumping up underneath it, Odysseus clung to its fleece. He twisted his arms and legs into the wool as the animal trotted toward Polyphemus.

"Oh, my ram," Polyphemus said, when he felt its horns. "Why are you last, instead of leading the way? What's the matter with you?"

He kept the ram in front of him, running his hands over it.

Underneath, Odysseus held his breath as the thick fingers came toward him. They were just about to touch his shoulder when Polyphemus stopped and let out a great sigh.

"You stayed behind because you're sad, didn't you, dear ram?" he said. "You know I've been hurt. If I could find Noe Boddy — that treacherous weakling — I would beat his brains out! Oh, if only you could tell me where he is!"

For a second he paused, almost as though he expected the ram to speak. Then he let it go, and it trotted out of the cave.

Odysseus loosened his cramped hands and jumped down. Quickly he untied his men, and they all raced toward their ship, herding the fat sheep with them. It would have been the perfect escape — if only Odysseus had kept his mouth shut.

But he didn't. As the ship left the shore, he ran to the stern and yelled triumphantly at Polyphemus.

"So I'm a treacherous weakling, am I, Cyclops? Well, this *weakling* has defeated you, and given you the punishment you deserve!"

The Cyclops heard his voice and charged toward the sea with a roar. Heaving a great rock out of the ground, he flung it into the sea, aiming toward the sound. The splash set the ship rocking, and the sailors pleaded with Odysseus to be quiet. But he wouldn't stop shouting.

44

"Do you want to know who was clever enough to trick you?" he yelled at Polyphemus. "Well, you can tell your friends it wasn't Noe Boddy. It was Odysseus, king of Ithaca!"

The Cyclops bellowed and lifted up his massive hands, calling out to the god Poseidon, who was his father. "Father Poseidon, grant me revenge! Stop Odysseus from reaching his home in Ithaca. Or, if he must reach home, let it be only after a long journey. Let him lose all his companions, and his ships, and arrive in Ithaca like a wretch, to find his home full of trouble!"

The sea swelled and thundered, boiling around Odysseus's ship. His men pulled at their oars, desperate to return to the island, where they had left their comrades and the other eleven ships. They were terrified of being wrecked before they could reach it.

But by morning they were there, and everything was calm. The sea slapped softly on the beach under a clear sky. It seemed that Polyphemus's curse had dissolved like a puff of wind.

But it hadn't. Deep under the River of Ocean, Poseidon, the earth shaker, had heard the voice of his son. Rearing up his mighty head, he scanned the wine-dark sea until he found Odysseus and his tiny fleet of twelve long ships. Shaking the tangled locks of his hair, Poseidon began to watch them.

AEOLUS AND CIRCE

ODYSSEUS HAD NO IDEA how much grief and suffering would come from his careless boast to Polyphemus. He and his men traveled on across the uncharted sea, congratulating themselves on their escape. They were still lost, but they let the wind carry them forward, hoping they would soon reach land.

It was a long time before the wind dropped. When it did, they saw an astonishing sight ahead of them.

They were close to an island — completely unlike any they had ever seen before. Its sides were tall cliffs, rising vertically out of the water. On top of the cliffs was an unbroken wall of bronze, running right around the island. The sailors stared up at it in astonishment. And, as they stared, they realized something even more amazing.

The island was floating.

It moved and shifted constantly on the surface of the water. Every gust of wind set it circling first one way and then another, drifting like a piece of thistledown.

The sailors muttered nervously to one another, wondering what kind of people might live on such an island. But Odysseus didn't hesitate. He stood at the prow of his ship and shouted up at the wall.

"I am Odysseus, king of Ithaca! My companions and I are on our way home from Troy. Are we welcome here?"

From behind the wall of bronze, a great voice boomed back at him. "You are welcome, Odysseus of Ithaca. Your ships have reached the home of Aeolus, Lord of the Winds. He invites you all to land here and refresh yourselves."

Rope ladders came snaking down from the top of the bronze wall, ready to be climbed. Immediately, Odysseus gave orders for all his ships to anchor. Lowering the boats, he and his men rowed over to the island and began to climb.

Aeolus was waiting for them inside the bronze wall. "Welcome to my home!" he said. "My wife and I live here with our six sons and their wives — who are also our daughters. We have everything we need on this beautiful island."

Inside his magnificent palace, a feast was already being prepared. He invited the visitors to share it, asking nothing in return except the story of their adventures.

The feast went on for a whole month. Aeolus listened eagerly to everything that Odysseus told him. He was full of questions, and Odysseus was happy to spend time answering them. His men needed a chance to relax and build up their strength.

But a month was enough. After that, Odysseus took Aeolus aside. "We must continue our journey," he said. "Will you help my ships on their way home to Ithaca?"

"With pleasure," said Aeolus. "I'll give you all the food and water you need—and a much greater gift as well."

He took out a huge leather bag, made of a whole ox skin, and held it up for Odysseus to see.

"Zeus has given me power over all the winds in the world," he said. "I will protect your ships and make sure that you have the right wind to blow you straight home."

Opening the bag, he filled it with all the fierce and dangerous winds that would have blown Odysseus off course and wrecked his ships. The bag swelled up, and he tied the top tightly with a silver wire. Then he stowed it in Odysseus's ship.

"Keep this safe until you reach your own island," he told Odysseus privately. "Don't open it—not even a crack—until you and all your men have landed there."

Only one wind had been left out of the bag. The gentle west wind that would take the ships home to Ithaca.

Odysseus and his men set sail at once. It was the easiest voyage any of them had ever made. For nine days, they sailed smoothly over a gentle sea, with blue sky above them and little waves lapping the sides of the ships. Odysseus was determined not to let anything go wrong this time. He insisted on steering his own ship all the way, without resting or sleeping.

On the tenth day, as the sun rose, they saw the rocky shape of Ithaca ahead of them on the horizon. Soon they were close enough to make out the glimmer of fires on the shore. They started to look forward to kissing their wives and hugging their children before the day was over.

But Odysseus was exhausted. He hadn't slept at all for nine days and nights. By the time the coast of Ithaca appeared, he was so tired that he couldn't keep his eyes open. Sinking down onto the deck, he fell fast asleep where he was — right beside the bulging ox-hide bag that Aeolus had given him.

For nine days, the sailors had been looking at the bag and wondering what was inside. Now they began to whisper about it.

"It's a great treasure," said one. "And Odysseus means to keep it all for himself."

"It's not fair!" said another. "We've been his companions all the way, and what have we got to give our wives? Nothing!"

The rest of them began to grumble too.

"He should share it with us. We've all suffered together."

"Why should he grab everything?"

"Let's take a look in the bag."

Without waking Odysseus, they hauled the huge, swollen skin out of its hiding place. They untwisted the wire that tied it shut, and opened the neck of the bag.

And all the wild winds in the world came raging out around them. Tornadoes and tempests tore into their sails. Gales and hurricanes drove the ships backward, flinging the sailors headlong onto the deck. They clung desperately to ropes and spars to stop themselves from being swept overboard — watching in despair

as the coast of Ithaca disappeared over the horizon. In the middle of this whirling storm, Odysseus woke up. Immediately he guessed what had happened, and all his hopes of seeing Penelope and Telemachus were ripped away. He was on the verge of throwing himself overboard. What was the point of struggling on? Why not just give up and drown? The temptation was strong — but his longing for Ithaca was even stronger. He curled into a ball, pulling his cloak right over his head.

Closing his eyes, he set himself to endure
the storm and the bitter disappointment.
After a long time, the winds blew themselves out
and the waves died down. Lifting his head, Odysseus
realized where they were. They had been blown
all the way back to the floating island of Aeolus.
Maybe that was a piece of good luck. Would
Aeolus help them again? For a second time,
Odysseus called up at the bronze wall above the
cliffs. But Aeolus was not welcoming this time. When
he heard what had happened, he reacted with cold fury.

"Get away from my island!" he shouted.
"The gods obviously detest you. I'm not going to
help a man they hate. Go away—and never come back!"
Odysseus and his men hoisted their sails, swamped by
despair. What fate was in store for them now? Would
they ever see their homes again?

BACK ON ITHACA, Penelope was

desperate for news. She questioned
every traveler who arrived on
the island, but no one could
tell her anything about
Odysseus. All she
could do was go on
waiting faithfully.

While she waited, Telemachus
was growing up. She talked to
him constantly about his father,
telling him what a clever, good
man Odysseus was.

"One day you'll see that for
yourself," she said. "One day
he'll come back."

Other people weren't so sure.
Men were beginning to look at
Penelope and see how beautiful she
was. "It's a waste," they muttered to
one another, "a waste for a woman
like that to wither away on her own.
She should choose another husband. . . ."

FAR AWAY FROM ITHACA, Odysseus and his men sailed on across the unknown, empty sea. As they sailed, they noticed the nights growing shorter and the days growing longer. And longer. And longer.

Finally, they reached a land where there was no night at all. Sunrise followed straight after sunset. As soon as the evening light started to fade, Dawn stretched her rosy fingers across the sky, turning it pink—and up came the sun again, not leaving any time for sleep and rest.

They had come to the land of the Laestrygonians.

If Odysseus had known what kind of people lived there, he would have ordered his sailors to row as hard as they could. He would have sent his ships racing away from shore.

But he didn't know. All he saw was a safe harbor, out of reach of the sea. It was formed by two long headlands curving around toward each other until they almost met. Their steep cliffs enclosed a circle of calm water large enough for all twelve of Odysseus's ships to anchor side by side.

Eleven of the ships sailed straight through the narrow gap between the headlands into the calm waters of the harbor.

But something held Odysseus back. He didn't understand why he was reluctant to follow the other ships, but he obeyed his instinct. Staying outside the harbor, he moored his ship to a rock at the end of one of the headlands. Then he clambered ashore and climbed up the hill to take a look inland.

There were no buildings in sight. No fields, no houses, no cattle. The only sign of any inhabitants was a single wisp of smoke.

He called three men ashore to join him. "Go and look for food and fresh water," he said. "And find out if there are any people living here."

The men set off at once, following a broad track that ran down from the hills. They hadn't gone far before they reached a spring of water. A large, strong girl was kneeling beside the spring, filling a jar. They greeted her politely and asked her where they were.

"You are in the land of my father, King Antiphates," she said. "He lives down there."

She stood up eagerly, pointing out her father's palace. They were startled by how big she was — she towered over all three of them — but she seemed friendly enough, so they went on toward the palace. It was a large, high building at the bottom of the hill, with a small town clustered around it.

When they entered the palace courtyard, Antiphates's wife came out to meet them. When the sailors saw her, they were terrified. She was a mountainous woman with arms like tree trunks and hands as big as hams.

But it was too late to escape. She called Antiphates, and he came charging out of the palace, licking his lips. He snatched up one of the sailors in a huge fist and grinned horribly.

"Supper!" he said.

59

The other two sailors ran for all they were worth, heading back toward the harbor. Antiphates ran after them, calling the rest of the Laestrygonians to join him.

Watching from his ship at the end of the headland, Odysseus saw the two men reappear, running for their lives. Close behind them came a crowd of giant Laestrygonians, howling with excitement.

Before Odysseus had time to react, the Laestrygonians were standing on top of the cliffs, hurling huge rocks down into the water. The eleven ships in the harbor splintered into pieces. Groaning and screaming, the injured sailors were thrown into the sea.

At once, the Laestrygonians slithered down the cliffs and waded into the water. They began to spear the drowning men as though they were fish.

There was no way of stopping the slaughter. All Odysseus could do was look after the men on his own ship. He drew his sword and sliced through the mooring rope, yelling at the top of his voice.

"Row! Row for your lives!"

Sobbing with grief and shock, the sailors pulled away from that hateful shore. The terrible screams of their comrades echoed in their ears.

They did not stop rowing for a second until the land of the Laestrygonians had disappeared and they were out in the wide, clean sea.

They had saved their own lives, but the other ships were lost, with all their crews. Odysseus had left Troy with twelve ships full of heroes heading back to Ithaca. Now there was only one ship left. And its sailors were weary and desperate and far from home.

The long ship limped across the sea, going wherever the current took it. The sailors were too shaken to care where they went.

When they reached land at last, there was none of the usual cheering or celebration. The ship slid silently into harbor, as if it had a crew of ghosts. The anchor dropped so slowly that the water around it barely rippled. When the sailors went ashore, they just lay on the beach for two days, so exhausted they couldn't move.

On the third day, Odysseus took his sword and spear and went off to explore. Scrambling up a hill, he saw that they were on a low, wooded island, thickly covered with trees and oak scrub.

The only open space was a clearing in the middle distance. Most of it was hidden behind tall trees, but he could see curls of reddish smoke between the branches. Obviously someone lived there.

He went back to the beach to collect his companions. "We need to find people who can tell us where we are," he said. "I've seen some smoke —"

Until he mentioned the smoke, the sailors had been numb with shock. Now they remembered the last wisps of smoke he'd spotted — and they began to relive the horrors they had seen in the land of the Laestrygonians. Men who had faced battles without flinching started to sob and wail, grieving for their dead comrades.

"We can't stay here!" they cried. "Or we'll meet more monsters!"

"How can we go?" said Odysseus. "We're completely lost. We have to find someone to tell us the way to Ithaca, otherwise we'll die without reaching home."

The men went on wailing and protesting, but Odysseus wouldn't listen. He divided them into two groups, one led by himself and the other by his mate Eurylochus. They drew lots to decide which group should go inland to explore, and Eurylochus's group was chosen. Still weeping, they set off into the forest, and Odysseus and the others settled down to wait for them.

There was no path to the clearing, so Eurylochus and his men had to cut their way through tangled undergrowth. Every time they heard a noise, Eurylochus insisted on stopping to look around. It was a long, slow journey.

Finally, they saw the open space ahead of them through the trees. They cut their way to the edge of the space and found themselves gazing at a fine stone house, built in the very center of the clearing. There was no one in sight. Cautiously, they took a step forward out of the trees.

At once, dark shapes raced out from behind the building. The sailors found themselves looking into open mouths with long, gleaming teeth.

Wolves and lions!

There was no time to run away. The men froze with fear, expecting to be torn to pieces by cruel fangs. Instead, the animals came crowding around them, nuzzling at their legs and licking their hands like tame dogs. Feeling as though they were in a dream, the sailors moved forward across the clearing.

Then they heard someone singing. From inside the house came the clack of a shuttle and the sound of a woman's voice. The most beautiful voice they had ever heard.

"Be careful," murmured Eurylochus under his breath. No one listened to him. All the other men were mesmerized by the singing.

"Is it a woman—or a goddess?" said Polites. He lifted his head and called toward the house.

"We are travelers who need help! Can you tell us where we are?"

There was a pause.

Then out of the house
came a woman with long,
flowing hair. She stood
in the doorway and smiled
at the staring sailors.

65

"Welcome," she said. "I am Circe. I can see that your journey has been long and exhausting. Come into my palace and eat with me. And rest." Her voice was like music, and the sunlight glinted in her hair.

"Be careful," Eurylochus muttered. "Very careful . . ."

The others didn't even hear him. They were already walking into the house, with their eyes on Circe's face, looking forward to the feast she had promised. Eurylochus hesitated for a second. Then he stepped back into the shelter of the trees. Fixing his eyes on the house, he waited to see if his companions would return.

Circe prepared a wonderful dish of cheese and barley meal and golden Pramnian wine. While it cooked, the sailors closed their eyes and breathed in the wonderful honey scent.

They didn't see the drug that Circe dropped into the pot.

When the barley meal was ready, she heaped it into bowls and set it on the long table in her banquet hall.

"Eat," she said, "and be refreshed."

It was delicious. The sailors ate it greedily, finishing every mouthful.

As they ate, their memories of Ithaca faded away. They forgot their homes and their families. All they thought about was spooning the food into their mouths, faster and faster and faster. Nothing else mattered. Guzzling down the barley meal, they changed from valiant men into . . .

"Pigs!" shouted Circe fiercely.

Her voice was not soft and welcoming now. She was holding a stick, and she beat them until they ran away from the table and out the back door of the house.

"You are pigs, not men!" she called after them. "Get off to the sty, where you belong!"

When they were all in the pigsty, she bolted the door and flung in handfuls of coarse, dry acorns for them to eat. They grunted wretchedly and snuffled in the straw with their damp, ugly snouts.

Though they had the bodies of pigs, their minds were still human. They wept as they ate the acorns.

Odysseus and his group of sailors knew nothing about all this until Eurylochus came running out of the forest. When they saw him, they were horrified. He was shaking all over and sobbing so hard that he couldn't speak.

And he was on his own.

"What happened to the others?" Odysseus said quickly. "Are they dead?"

Eurylochus couldn't speak. He just shuddered and covered his face with his hands.

They sat him beside the fire and wrapped a cloak around his shoulders, and at last he calmed down enough to start talking. He described the house in the clearing and the beautiful singing.

"I warned them to be careful," he said. "But when Circe invited them in, they didn't listen to me. They all followed her — and that was the last time I saw them."

Odysseus frowned. "Didn't you look for them?"

"Yes, I did," Eurylochus said miserably. "After a long time, I crept over to the house and peered inside. The banquet hall was deserted, and the chairs were tumbled on the floor. Circe must have killed them all. Let's get away from here!"

"Not until we know what's happened to our comrades," Odysseus said firmly. "Show me the way to Circe's house."

Eurylochus fell to his knees. "Please don't force me back to that terrible place! We can't rescue the others. We must think of ourselves and sail away from here!"

Odysseus saw how distressed he was. "Stay here with the other men," he said. "They'll take care of you. I'm going to Circe's house to find out what she's done to our companions. That's my duty."

Leaving Eurylochus with the rest of the crew, he set off on his own down the newly made path. He'd almost reached Circe's palace when suddenly, out of nowhere, a young man appeared on the path in front of him.

"Where are you going?" he said to Odysseus. "Are you off to Circe's house to rescue your poor sailors from her pigsty?"

Odysseus stared at him.

The young man smiled. "You'll find yourself in the pigsty too," he said, "unless you accept my protection." He reached out his hand, and Odysseus saw that he was holding a strange plant with a black root and a flower as white as milk.

It was moly.

No human being would have dared to dig up such a dangerous plant. Staring down at it, Odysseus knew that the young man in front of him was no mortal. He was Hermes, the giant killer and messenger of the gods.

Odysseus bowed his head and listened carefully to the god's instructions.

"Circe will make you a drugged meal," Hermes said. "But this plant will rob the drug of its power and protect you from her evil spells. Eat what she gives you, and wait until she strikes you with her wand. Then draw your sword and threaten to kill her — and she will obey your orders."

He dropped the plant into Odysseus's hand and disappeared.

Slipping a leaf of moly under his tongue, Odysseus continued down the path. Circe's magic glade was only a little way further on. He strode into it, calling out boldly, "Who's there? Is there any welcome for a weary traveler?"

Circe came through the polished doors of her house and looked at him across the clearing. Raising one white hand, she beckoned to him.

Warily, Odysseus followed her into the house. She waved him toward a beautiful, silver-studded chair and pulled up a stool for his feet.

"Rest there," she said sweetly. "You must be tired after your journey. Let me prepare a drink to revive you."

She went out and came back with a golden bowl in her hands. Odysseus put it to his lips, and she watched until he'd drunk it all to the last drop.

Then she lifted her stick and hit him on the shoulder.

"Be off to the pigsty with your friends!" she said scornfully.

But Odysseus didn't change his shape as she was expecting. He still had the moly leaf under his tongue. Jumping up, he drew his sword and charged at her as though he meant to kill her.

Circe shrieked and flung herself onto her knees. "Who are you? How could you drink my drug without being affected?"

She clasped Odysseus's feet and burst into tears. In her terror, she was prepared to do anything to save her life.

"Do you think I'm beautiful? If you spare my life, I will be your lover and you will find me faithful and true. Put your sword down and be gentle."

"How can I be gentle when my friends are in the pigsty?" Odysseus said curtly. "I won't put my sword away until you swear, by all the gods, not to harm anyone else."

Circe swore it, solemnly. Then she ordered her maids to prepare a feast. But Odysseus refused to eat.

"How can I feast until my men are free? If you really want to win my heart, bring them here and undo your spell."

Circe didn't hesitate. She went straight to the pigsty and unlocked the door. With her stick in her hand, she drove the pigs into the banquet hall. Then she smeared each of them with a magic ointment. One by one, as she rubbed it over their bristly skins, they changed back into the men Odysseus knew.

Their memories came back as well. As they recognized Odysseus, they began to weep tears of such happiness that even Circe's heart was touched.

"Noble Odysseus," she said, "bring the rest of your sailors here and I will prepare a feast for you all. Then I will tell you how to find your way home. You can trust me. Remember what I have sworn."

Odysseus knew that she would not dare to break that oath. So he went back to the shore and led the rest of his sailors to Circe's palace. Even Eurylochus was persuaded to forget his fear and join them.

Circe prepared such a magnificent feast that they stayed in her house for a whole year, recovering from their grief and exhaustion. They spent all the winter there, but when the long summer days came back, the sailors took Odysseus aside.

"It's time to go home," they said.

Odysseus knew they were right. At the end of that day's feasting, he went to Circe and reminded her of her promise to help them.

"We want to leave at once," he said. "Which is the way to Ithaca?"

"It's not enough to know the right direction," Circe said gravely. "Before you sail, you must consult the soul of Tiresias, the prophet, in the Land of the Dead."

"The Land of the Dead?" Odysseus was appalled. "No one has ever sailed there. How can a ship reach such a place?"

GHOSTS AND MONSTERS

ODYSSEUS SPENT MOST OF THE NIGHT listening to Circe's instructions. At dawn the next morning, he woke his men and ordered them to get ready for the voyage. Hastily they left Circe's house and headed down to the shore to prepare their ship.

All except Elpenor.

He had drunk too much wine the night before. Then, because he was hot, he'd climbed onto the roof of Circe's palace and fallen asleep there. When he heard Odysseus calling the sailors together, he woke up suddenly. Forgetting where he was, he jumped to his feet — and fell off the roof. His neck broke and he died instantly.

None of the others noticed what had happened. They were all listening in amazement to what Odysseus was saying.

"We cannot sail for Ithaca yet," he told them. "First we have to go to the Land of the Dead to ask advice from the prophet Tiresias."

The sailors were afraid, but they obeyed his orders. As they pushed their ship out into the water, Circe came down to the shore with a ram and a black ewe.

"Remember," she said to Odysseus, "you must sail until you find a grove of poplars and long-leaved willow trees. When you see that, you must walk inland and sacrifice these animals where the two rivers meet, as I told you." She drove the sheep on board and then lifted her staff and waved it in the air, calling up the north wind they needed.

All day they sailed across the wine-dark sea. As night fell, they reached a wild coast and saw a single grove of poplars and willows, exactly as Circe had foretold. Pulling their ship onto the beach, they walked inland, driving the sheep ahead of them.

Soon, they saw a steep, rocky pinnacle looming up in the darkness. That marked the place where the River of Flaming Fire joined the River of Lamentation. Together, they flowed into the great, black Acheron that ran through the Land of the Dead.

RIVER OF LAMENTATION

"This is where we must sacrifice the sheep," Odysseus said. "When they smell the blood, the souls of the dead will rise up to meet us, and we will ask them to bring Tiresias." Following Circe's instructions, he poured honey and milk into a trench, adding wine and water and grains of barley. Then he sacrificed the sheep and drew his sword. The souls of the dead came fluttering up from the underworld with hollow, eerie cries. Thousands of them flocked around Odysseus as he stood shivering on the edge of the trench. The ghosts of young men and girls floated next to battle-scarred warriors. Old men with gray hair brushed against newly married brides. They jostled together, vying for Odysseus's attention. He scanned their insubstantial faces — and suddenly he recognized one. "Elpenor! How can you be here, among the dead?"

"I fell from the roof and broke my neck," Elpenor said mournfully. "My body is lying behind Circe's palace. Please go back and give me a proper funeral."

"I will," promised Odysseus. "But first I must speak to the prophet Tiresias."

ACHERON

RIVER OF FLAMING FIRE

77

"There he is," Elpenor said, "coming toward us now."

Odysseus turned and saw the shade of the old, blind prophet rising through the darkness. He stepped forward respectfully, waiting for Tiresias to speak.

"Noble Odysseus," said Tiresias, "I know your heart's desire is to return to Ithaca. But you have angered Poseidon. Because you blinded the Cyclops, his son, he will make your journey as difficult as he can."

"Are you saying we shall never reach home?" Odysseus cried.

"There is a chance for you all," Tiresias said. "But only if you keep your men under control. When you reach the island of Thrinacia, don't let your men touch the sun god's cattle. If they hurt those cattle, your ship will be lost. And all your sailors, too."

"What about me?" said Odysseus.

"You may survive. But if you do, I prophesy that it will be many years before you reach Ithaca. And when you do, you will enter your house in rags, and find it full of trouble."

"Will Poseidon be satisfied with that?" Odysseus asked.

Tiresias shook his great head sadly. "If you want to be free of Poseidon's curse, you must make another journey. Travel inland with an oar over your shoulder, until you are far away from the sea. When someone mistakes your oar for a winnowing fan, sacrifice to Poseidon there. Then he will let you live in peace again."

Bowing his head, Tiresias drifted back into the underworld. Then all the other shades swirled around Odysseus in a cloud of familiar and unfamiliar faces, chanting their stories to him.

But the spirits of the dead cannot stay long in the world of the living. One by one they dwindled away, until Odysseus and his men were on their own beside the thundering rivers.

With heavy hearts, they returned to their ship and let the wind carry them back to Circe's island. There, at dawn, they built a funeral pyre for their friend Elpenor and cremated him, with all his weapons. When his ashes were cold, they built a mound on the seashore, so that his name would never be forgotten.

After the funeral, Circe and her handmaidens came down to the shore, carrying bread and meat and sparkling red wine.

"You are heroes," Circe said. "You have been to the Land of the Dead and back again. Spend the rest of the day here, feasting with me, and I will tell you about all the dangers ahead, so that you are ready to face them when you sail tomorrow."

All day they feasted, until sunset. As night began to fall, the sailors settled down to sleep beside the ship. Then Circe took Odysseus by the hand and led him to a place where they could talk privately.

"You are going to sail into many dangers," she said. "First you will come to the Sirens, whose song drives men mad with longing. If you succeed in passing them, you will reach the Wandering Rocks. They wreck every ship that approaches. You must avoid them — but you can only do that by facing a terrible choice. Listen carefully to everything I tell you, Odysseus. . . ."

Far into the night they sat together, and Circe talked on and on, warning Odysseus about what lay ahead.

In the morning, Odysseus woke his men and ordered them onto the ship. Circe gave them a favorable wind, and they set sail immediately. When they were safely out at sea, Odysseus told them the first of Circe's warnings.

"A great danger lies ahead of us," he said. "Soon we shall come to the place where the Sirens sing. Everyone who hears them wants to go on listening forever. Unless you close your ears to the sound, you will never reach home, never see your wives and children again."

He lifted a ball of beeswax that Circe had given him, working it in his fingers as he spoke.

"I shall block your ears with this to protect you. But not my own. I am determined to hear the Sirens sing, and Circe has told me the only way to do that safely. When I have filled your ears with wax, you must tie me to the mast. Knot the ropes tightly, so that I can't move. And if I beg you to let me go — just pull them even tighter."

As he spoke, the wind dropped and the ship came to a standstill. The sailors looked at one another. They would never get past the Sirens unless they kept rowing.

Odysseus went around the ship, plugging their ears with wax. When he had finished, the sailors fetched ropes and lashed him to the mast so tightly that he couldn't move hand or foot. Then they took up their oars and began to row as hard as they could.

Very soon they drew up to a flowery meadow that ran beside the seashore. That was where the Sirens sat — surrounded by the skeletons of all those who had stayed to listen to their song.

As soon as they saw Odysseus's ship, they began to sing again, turning their heads so that the sound floated out over the water.

Come here to us and stop your restless journey, they sang.
Come here and listen to the sound of wisdom,
To all the gathered knowledge of the world
Distilled into the music of our song.
Come here to us . . . come here to us . . . come here to us . . .

That was the song Odysseus heard. It filled him with such longing that he shouted to his men to put down their oars and untie him. When they did not answer — because they couldn't hear — he screamed and ranted, rolling his eyes and making anguished faces.

"Undo the ropes!" he shrieked. "Everything I said before was nonsense. Everything is nonsense except the Sirens' song. Stop rowing! Let me go to them!"

If he'd been free, he would have jumped overboard and swum to the shore. But he couldn't move — and the sailors obeyed the instructions he'd given them. Two men jumped up and tightened the cords that held him to the mast. The others kept rowing, pulling with all their strength. Some of them were tempted to

84

stop and unblock their ears. They had been away from home
for more than ten years now, and Ithaca seemed very far away.
But they were faithful to Odysseus's orders. Closing their eyes
to shut out the sight of his desperate, yearning face, they leaned
into their oars and pulled . . . and pulled . . . and pulled. . . .

85

FOR MORE THAN TEN YEARS,

Penelope had been staring at the horizon, watching for Odysseus's ships. How long should a loyal wife wait?

"Suppose he never comes back?"

Now people were asking the question openly. All over Ithaca and beyond, men talked about beautiful, wise Penelope and wondered who would be her second husband.

The only person who never wondered was Penelope herself. "I am Odysseus's wife," she said. "And I am Telemachus's mother. I will not even think of marrying again until Telemachus is a man."

Her determination kept the suitors away for the time being. But still there was no sign of the twelve long ships that had sailed to Troy.

And Telemachus kept on growing. . . .

OUT ON THE WINE-DARK SEA, the one remaining ship sailed on, away from the land of the Sirens.

As soon as their song faded away in the distance, Odysseus stopped shouting and struggling. When the sailors saw that, they jumped up and ran to untie him, pulling the wax out of their ears.

"Thank you for your loyalty," Odysseus said. "You are faithful friends. Now I must tell you —"

But before he could finish, a great cloud of spray erupted ahead of them, shooting into the sky. There was a thunderous crash of water breaking against rocks. The sailors gasped in terror, and Odysseus stared at the spray, with Circe's next warning echoing in his head.

If you succeed in passing the Sirens, you will reach the Wandering Rocks. They wreck every ship that approaches. You must avoid them — but you can only do that by facing a terrible choice.

They had to avoid that violent, crashing water. But the only other route was a narrow strait between two rocky peaks. How could he tell his sailors about the dangers lurking at each one? They had just saved his life by their faithfulness. Now, according to Circe, all he had to offer them was a choice of death — or death.

Scylla or Charybdis.

A monster or a whirlpool.

Scylla's lair was a cave, high up in the taller rock. Every time a ship went past, her six long necks swooped down. Each of her six hungry heads snatched up one of the sailors and ate him.

The ships that tried to avoid her steered close to the other rock and fell into the great whirlpool called Charybdis. That meant certain death. Three times a day the whirlpool's greedy mouth opened up, sucking in everything around it. Three times a day it changed direction, spewing everything up again. The force was enough to smash any ship and destroy its crew.

Steer close to Scylla's rock, Circe had said. *And row as fast as you can. Even so, you're bound to lose six men — but that's better than having your whole crew swallowed up by Charybdis.*

There was no other way. Odysseus didn't dare to tell his men the whole truth, in case they were so terrified that they stopped rowing. He told them only half.

"We have to sail between those two rocky peaks," he said, pointing at the entrance to the narrow strait. "But we must be very careful. Do you see the fig tree growing on the smaller rock? Below that is a gigantic whirlpool. We must stay away from that."

He took his sword and stood on the prow of the ship, watching the way ahead. The sailors rowed nervously, looking toward the fig tree. As they passed it, the sea underneath began to swirl and boil. A vast hole opened up in the surface of the water, sucking in everything around it. The sailors pulled on their oars, pale with terror, staying as far away from the hole as possible.

And that was when Scylla struck.

Her ugly heads came shooting out of the cave, darting down toward the sailors. She snatched up the six strongest men and hoisted them into the air.

"Odysseus!" they screamed. "Save us, Odysseus!"

What could he do? There was no way of reaching Scylla's cave. He had to watch his faithful companions dangling from her fangs like fish from a line. The monstrous heads reared up, snaking back toward her lair, and for a short time, the sailors' screams echoed horribly over the water. Then there was silence.

"Row on!" said Odysseus fiercely. "Row on, as fast as you can!"

There was nothing else to do.

89

As they went through the strait, Scylla and Charybdis vanished in the distance and a new island appeared on the horizon. As they came closer, they saw that it was completely different from the horrors behind them.

Streams of clear, fresh water gleamed golden in the evening light. Rich, green grassland spread inland from the shore. Across the sea came the sound of cattle lowing contentedly as they were taken in for the night.

To the grieving, exhausted sailors, the island looked like paradise. They imagined themselves rowing ashore, and they could almost smell the wonderful scent of freshly roasted meat.

But Odysseus remembered the words of the blind prophet, Tiresias, in the Land of the Dead.

When you reach the island of Thrinacia, don't let your men touch the sun god's cattle. If they hurt those cattle, your ship will be lost. And all your sailors, too.

Listening to the sound of the cattle across the water, he guessed that the island ahead was Thrinacia. "We mustn't land here," he said. "Tiresias warned me about this place — and so did Circe. It belongs to the sun god. We must find somewhere else to anchor."

There was an uproar.

"Are you made of iron?" Eurylochus said. "Do you think we can go on rowing forever? Where's the harm in landing here, just for the night? All we want is the chance to step ashore and eat one meal without tossing around on the water."

The other men shouted in agreement. They insisted that Odysseus change his mind and let them spend the night on dry land. At last he nodded reluctantly.

"Very well. But you must swear not to kill anything on the island. Not one cow or a single sheep."

The men swore a solemn oath, promising to stay close to the ship and to eat nothing except the food Circe had given them. Trusting to that oath, Odysseus let them steer the ship into a sheltered cove. They went ashore and ate a silent meal, not talking or telling jokes, but remembering their dead companions, snatched away by Scylla.

They slept beside the ship, intending to go on board again as soon as it was light. But in the middle of the night, a fierce gale blew up, whipping the water into huge breakers. In the morning there was no hope of setting sail. All they could do was drag their ship up into a cave to keep it safe from the storm.

Sternly, Odysseus reminded them of their promise. "Remember, you are not to touch any of the cows or sheep on this island. They all belong to the Sun, that great god whose eye sees everything."

For a second time, the sailors swore to leave the animals alone.

They meant it. They had plenty of bread and wine aboard the ship, and they didn't expect to be on the island for more than a few days.

But then the wind changed.

For a whole month the south wind blew continuously, driving the sea against the shore. It was impossible to launch a ship. They had to stay where they were — and they began to run out of food.

When their own food was gone, the sailors began to roam the island, trapping birds and catching fish. But, however much they hunted, there was never enough to stop them from feeling hungry.

And the hungrier they grew, the more they looked at the sun god's cattle.

Odysseus saw them looking and knew there would be trouble if they didn't leave soon. But the wind was still blowing in the wrong direction, and only the gods could alter that. One morning, he left his sailors on the shore and walked inland on his own. Finding a lonely, sheltered place, he prayed to all the gods on Olympus, asking for a change in the wind. He prayed so long and so earnestly that, in the end, he fell asleep. In that hidden place, out of reach of the wind, he slept peacefully for several hours.

Back on the beach, the sailors were muttering together while he slept.

"We can't go on like this," Eurylochus said. "Odysseus threatens us with disaster if we touch the sun god's cattle — but what's more disastrous than starving to death? If we don't eat soon, we'll be too weak to sail away, even if the wind does change."

The sailors hesitated, remembering their oath.

Eurylochus argued harder, to persuade them. "Let's choose the best of these cows and sacrifice them to the gods. Then we'll have plenty of meat to eat. If we get back to Ithaca afterward, we'll build a splendid temple for the sun god, to repay him for his cattle."

"But we won't get home," said one of the other sailors. "Not if we kill the cattle."

Eurylochus shrugged. "Wouldn't you rather drown than starve to death?"

That convinced the others. As soon as he finished speaking, they rounded up the best cattle and sacrificed them ceremonially.

Then they built a fire on the beach to roast the meat.

HIGH ON MOUNT OLYMPUS, the gods heard
the angry voice of Hyperion, the sun god. "O Father Zeus!" he
cried, "Odysseus's men have killed my beautiful cattle! Give
me revenge! Otherwise I'll go down to the Land of the Dead
and shine there, leaving the world dark forever."

94

"Peace, Hyperion," said Zeus, the cloud gatherer. "Stay
where you are — and leave those cattle murderers to me.
As soon as their ship is out at sea, I will strike it with a
lightning bolt and smash it to pieces."

95

WHEN ODYSSEUS WOKE UP, he started back toward the beach. He hadn't gone very far when he smelled the scent of roasting meat. He guessed what had happened, and he ran the rest of the way.

"What have you done?" he shouted. "Do you think the gods are blind?"

The guilty sailors hung their heads, but the harm was done. It was too late to bring the cows back to life. All they could do was wait for the gods to punish them.

They were surrounded by terrifying sights. The empty cowhides hunched themselves up and crawled about on the beach. The meat that was roasting on spits bellowed over the fire. And from all sides, day and night, came the baleful lowing of ghostly cattle.

For six days, the sailors had to live with what they had done, eating the stolen meat and waiting for the justice of the gods.

On the seventh day, the south wind dropped at last. Pushing their ship into the water, they embarked as fast as they could, rowing away from the beach with all their strength. Very quickly, the island disappeared over the horizon.

But they couldn't escape the anger of Zeus. When they were out in the open sea, a black cloud appeared from nowhere and settled over their ship. All around them, sunlight glinted on the water, but their ship was in darkness, overshadowed by the cloud.

Then, without warning, a savage wind roared in from the west. It hit the ship like a hurricane, snapping both forestays. The mast came crashing down in a tangle of sails and rigging, breaking the helmsman's skull. As he slid overboard, there was a great crack of thunder. A bolt of lightning shook the ship, and everyone was thrown into the sea.

The sailors had no chance of surviving in the wild water. One by one they were overwhelmed by the waves, until their bodies floated around the ruined hull like a flock of seabirds. There would be no joyful homecoming for any of them. Their voyage was over, forever.

Only Odysseus managed to stay alive. As the waves tore the ship apart, he seized a leather rope and tied the mast and the keel board together. Clinging tightly to those two pieces of wood, he kept himself afloat as the hurricane drove him through the water.

But he couldn't steer his makeshift raft. All night he was thrown from one wave to another, helpless as the wind blew him back toward Scylla and Charybdis. When Dawn spread her rosy fingers across the sky, Odysseus was in the narrow strait again, being swept toward the two sharp rocks.

The water below the fig tree was beginning to spin as Charybdis prepared to open its greedy mouth. Odysseus had no way of avoiding the whirlpool. There was only one possible chance of escape — if he was brave enough to take it.

As his tiny raft reached the fig tree, he stood up and grabbed at its nearest branch, high above his head. His hands closed around it, but without a foothold, he couldn't swing himself up into the tree. All he could do was cling on, hanging by his arms. Beneath him, the water spun faster and faster. With a horrible, greedy gurgle, it opened up into a black hole that went right down into the depths of the sea. Dangling above it, Odysseus saw it swallow his raft. Then it gaped open again, waiting for him to get tired and lose his grip.

Somehow he managed not to let go. Hour after hour he held on, watching the whirlpool below him, waiting for the moment when it began to spin the other way. The sun set, and as the sky grew dark, the direction of the water changed. Charybdis began to spew up everything it had swallowed.

Odysseus hung on, waiting to see his raft reappear.

As soon as the long timbers surfaced, he unclenched his stiff hands and dropped into the water. For a second he was in its power, spinning wildly. Then he hauled himself onto the raft and lay flat out, slumped across the wood.

Paddling furiously with both hands, he pulled himself away from the whirlpool as fast as he could, terrified that Scylla would catch sight of him. If she'd seen him, she would have snatched him up in a single mouthful. But it was almost dark, and the evening shadows hid him from her eyes. He came safely out of the perilous strait and into the open sea.

STRANDED ON CALYPSO'S ISLAND

FOR NINE DAYS, ODYSSEUS WAS ON HIS own in the ocean, drifting without food or fresh water. On the tenth day, he was washed up, like a piece of flotsam, on the shore of a lonely island.

He had landed on Ogygia, the home of the goddess Calypso. She found him lying weak and exhausted on the beach, and she treated him kindly. Taking him into her house, she fed him and nursed him back to health. It might have been the end of all his troubles, except for one thing.

Calypso fell in love with him.

Her love was relentless. She prepared great feasts for him, gave him sumptuous robes, and arranged spectacular entertainments to amuse him. Every day she offered to give him anything his heart desired — except the one thing he really wanted.

She wouldn't let him leave her island.

Odysseus was wretched. He pined for his home, for his wife and son and his own rocky island of Ithaca. He wasn't interested in any of Calypso's gifts. Day after day, he went down to the seashore and looked out over the ocean, longing to sail away. But what can a mortal man do against a goddess? All he could do was dream of going home.

Day after day.

Year after year after year . . .

In Ithaca, too,

the years were passing by. Telemachus grew older and taller, until he was almost as strong as his father. Penelope was proud of him, but soon he would be a man — and then what would happen to her?

Other people were watching Telemachus. When he was seventeen, men began visiting the palace as suitors, urging Penelope to choose a new husband. She did not want to marry any of them, but they were guests, and she had a duty to entertain them.

They exploited her hospitality. Day after day they feasted and drank at her expense, flirting with her maids and insulting her menservants. More and more suitors came, until there were more than a hundred of them. They took over her house.

"Telemachus has grown up," they kept saying, "and it's obvious that Odysseus will never return. You must marry one of us."

Desperately, Penelope found another excuse. "I can't marry yet," she said. "Odysseus's father is an old man, and he'll die soon. But I haven't woven a shroud fit to wrap his body in. I can't marry anyone until I've done that."

Grudgingly the suitors accepted her excuse. But they made her promise solemnly that once the shroud was finished, she would choose a new husband.

So Penelope began to weave, watching the sea as she sat at her loom and straining her eyes for a glimpse of Odysseus's ship. She was determined not to finish the shroud before he came home.

So she wove all day, but night after night, when the suitors had gone home, she crept out of bed and went back to her loom. Carefully she unpicked everything she had woven that day.

But how long could she keep that up before they discovered her trick?

Where *was* Odysseus?

HESTIA APHRODITE APOLLO HERMES ATHENE ZEUS

THE GODS WERE

THE GODS WERE WATCHING HIM. Looking down from the heights of Mount Olympus, they saw him on Calypso's island. His misery touched the heart of Athene, the goddess with the flashing eyes.

"Father Zeus," she said, "Odysseus has always worshipped you. Why are you so unkind to him?"

"I haven't caused his troubles," Zeus replied. "They come from Poseidon, the earth shaker. He is taking revenge for the blinding of his son the Cyclops."

106

"Odysseus has suffered enough!" Athene said passionately.

"He has," said Zeus. "And now Poseidon is busy on the other side of the world. Let us decide how to send Odysseus home."

Athene already had a plan. "Send Hermes to see Calypso," she said. "Order her to let Odysseus go — and to help him on his way."

"Very well," said Zeus. And he called Hermes over to give him the message.

Riding the waves like a seagull hunting fish, Hermes traveled over the blue waters of the sea to Calypso's island. He found Calypso at home in her cave, weaving with a golden shuttle.

She recognized Hermes at once—but she wasn't expecting the message he brought. When she heard Zeus's orders, she shuddered.

"You gods are so hard-hearted!" she said bitterly. "You cannot bear a goddess to choose a mortal husband. I saved Odysseus from shipwreck and took him into my home. I've even offered to make him immortal. How can I send him away now?"

"Those are Zeus's orders," Hermes said. "Do you want to rouse his anger?"

Calypso knew she had to obey. Sadly she went down to the seashore to find Odysseus. He was there, as usual, sitting on the rocks and weeping as he looked toward Ithaca. When she saw him, her heart was touched with pity.

"You need not cry anymore," she said. "I'll help you travel home. I can give you materials to make a raft, and warm clothes and food for your journey."

She fetched a great ax of bronze and an adze of polished metal. Then she led Odysseus to the other end of the island, where the trees grew tallest. He set to work at once, felling trees and splitting them into planks.

It took him four days to build the raft. He gave it a mast and fitted it with a rudder for steering. When it was ready, he dragged it down to the sea on rollers and Calypso gave him wine, water, a leather sack of grain, and a store of roasted meat.

"Keep the constellation of Orion on your left," she said, "if you want to get back to Ithaca."

Odysseus thanked her for all she had done for him and then launched his raft with a happy heart. Hoisting the sail, he set off in the direction Calypso had shown him, determined to reach home this time.

For seventeen days and nights, he traveled without sleeping, steering by the sun and the stars. At dawn on the eighteenth day, he saw shadowy mountains on the horizon. Joyfully, he recognized the outline of the Phaeacian coast.

He was almost home!

But he was still on the sea. And as Odysseus stared at the mountains, Poseidon noticed his tiny raft bobbing along in the vast ocean. When he saw Odysseus on his way to Ithaca, he flew into a rage.

"Miserable wretch!" he bellowed. "Do you think you've escaped my anger? See what happens to those who offend Poseidon!"

Stirring the sea into a fury with his trident, he called up huge black clouds to cover the sky. All the winds of heaven clashed together, unleashing their strength, and the ocean gathered itself into a towering wall of water.

Odysseus looked up in terror at the monstrous wave rolling toward his raft. How could he survive such an onslaught?

"Why wasn't I killed at Troy?" he shouted in despair. "That would have been a hero's death. The Greeks would have given me an honorable funeral and remembered my story forever. Now I'm doomed to die alone in this terrible storm."

Before he'd finished speaking, the great wave came crashing down onto his fragile raft. It spun out of control as the fierce winds snapped its mast in two, and Odysseus was thrown overboard into the dark salt sea.

111

Down and down he went, dragged under by the weight of water soaking into his clothes. Desperately he struggled out of them. Then he swam upward as hard as he could, with his lungs bursting.

When he reached the surface, he found the wild storm still raging. Great waves crashed into him, and savage winds battered his face. It was impossible to stay alive for more than a few minutes in such a sea.

But his raft was still afloat, tossing on the waves. Its sail and rudder had gone and it was beginning to break up, but it was his only hope. Fighting his way toward it, he clambered on board, clinging to the splintered planks.

The sea flung him backward and forward, thundering into him from every side. He had no way of defending himself from the force of the water. Closing his eyes, he waited for it to overwhelm him.

But someone was watching him. From under the water, a pair of eyes was following every movement of the raft.

It was Ino, of the slender ankles, a goddess who lived in the salt depths of the sea. She was once a mortal woman, and she knew what it was to suffer. Taking pity on Odysseus, she rose out of the water and settled on his raft like a seagull.

"Poor man," she said. "Poseidon is your enemy. He is trying to kill you. Leave your raft behind and swim as fast as you can to the Phaeacian shore. You will be safe there."

"I'll drown," Odysseus said.

Ino shook her head. "Not if I help you. Take my veil and wind it around your waist. It will protect you from injury and death. But you must not keep it after you reach the shore. The moment your hands touch dry land, you must untie it and throw it into the sea. Turn your eyes away as you throw it, and it will come back to me." Pressing the veil into his hands, she sank back under the raging sea.

Odysseus looked at it suspiciously. Could he trust Ino? Or was she another deceiver, like Circe, tempting him to leave his raft? Wasn't it more sensible to stay on board?

Before he could decide, Poseidon whipped up another giant wave. It raced toward him, heavy and menacing, and smashed down onto the raft, knocking it to pieces. Odysseus just managed to catch hold of one plank, straddling it to keep himself afloat.

He had nothing now. No possessions, no clothes, not even a raft. His only hope was Ino's veil. Tying it around his waist, he threw himself headfirst into the sea.

Poseidon snorted scornfully and abandoned him to the waves. He had stripped him of everything, and he was satisfied at last.

For two days and nights, Odysseus was alone in the wild water. The sea was so rough that he couldn't see beyond the nearest wave. Over and over again, he thought he was going to die.

He didn't die. Ino's veil kept him afloat, and the sea drove him steadily toward the Phaeacian coast. On the third day, the wind dropped and he found himself in a calm sea with waves that swelled slowly, carrying him toward the shore.

It was not a welcoming coast. The sea smashed against jagged reefs and sheer cliffs, boiling up in clouds of spray. It threw Odysseus against the rocks, and he would have been seriously injured if he hadn't grabbed one of them to hold himself back.

The next moment, the sea retreated, knocking his hands loose and leaving them skinned and bleeding. He forced himself to keep swimming, working his way along the coastline in search of an easier place to land.

IT WAS NOT A WELCOMING COAST. THE SEA SMASHED AGAINST JAGGED REEFS

At last he came to the mouth of a swiftly running stream. Struggling up the stream, he hauled himself onto the bank, out of reach of the waves. He was utterly exhausted, but he had one more thing to do before he could rest.

Untying Ino's veil from his waist, he dropped it into the water, turning his eyes away. It was swept off downstream and carried out to sea, back to its gentle owner.

After that effort, Odysseus had barely enough strength to find a hiding place. Naked and vulnerable as he was, he crawled up the riverbank and into the woods. Curling up under an olive tree, he covered himself with a blanket of fallen leaves and fell fast asleep.

LOOKING DOWN on Ithaca, Athene saw that it was time for Telemachus to go traveling too — now that he was a man.

She disguised herself as an old family friend and appeared outside the palace in Ithaca. The whole place was in chaos, with drunken suitors overrunning the hall while Telemachus sat gloomily in a corner.

But he didn't forget his manners. When he saw Athene, he jumped up to welcome her.

"What's going on?" Athene said, looking around at the rowdy suitors. "I've never seen anything so disorderly. Odysseus wouldn't have allowed behavior like this."

"If only he were here!" Telemachus said. "What's happened to him? Why doesn't he come home?"

"Maybe you should go and find out," Athene said softly. "The other Greek kings came back long ago. They might have news of your father — but you would have to sail across the sea to ask them. Are you brave enough for that?"

"Yes, I am!" Telemachus said fiercely. "I'm as brave as my father. But my mother has forbidden me to go."

"Then don't tell her," said Athene bluntly. "Just take a ship and sail away. She'll forgive you if you come back with news of Odysseus."

Telemachus knew she was right. Quietly, with her help, he began to make preparations to sail. When the ship was ready, with all the crew on board, he told just one person what he was doing — his old nurse, Eurycleia.

"I am going to Sparta, to see King Menelaus," he said. "You must swear not to tell my mother until my ship is safely out at sea."

Eurycleia shrieked and cried, but she promised to keep the secret.

Before she nursed Telemachus, she had been Odysseus's nurse, and she longed for news of him.

Telemachus set sail after sunset, slipping away from Ithaca in the dark. When Penelope heard what he'd done, she was distraught.

"Now I've lost my son as well as my husband," she said. She shut herself up in her room and cried inconsolably.

But the suitors were delighted to hear what Telemachus was doing.

"This is our chance!" they said to one another. "He'll have to sail back past the island of Asteris. Let's send a ship there — and ambush him! We'll kill him, so that Penelope has to marry one of us. And if Telemachus is dead, the man she marries will have the kingdom, too."

Greedily, they began to plot the murder.

NAUSICAA

‖‖‖‖‖‖‖‖‖‖‖‖‖‖‖‖‖‖‖‖‖‖‖‖‖‖‖‖‖‖‖‖‖‖‖‖

IN THE LAND OF THE PHAEACIANS, while Odysseus slept, the goddess Athene was at work, planning his rescue. She knew exactly the right person to help him — beautiful Nausicaa, the daughter of the Phaeacian king.

Athene made her way to King Alcinous's palace and found Nausicaa sleeping in her room. Two maids were asleep by the door to guard against intruders, but Athene wafted past them and through the closed doors like a puff of wind.

Disguising herself as one of Nausicaa's friends, she hovered over the princess's bed and whispered into her dreams.

"Look at your room, Nausicaa! Dirty clothes all over the floor! You'll never find a husband if you're so untidy. Get your father to lend us a wagon in the morning and we'll go down to the river and do some washing. Then you'll be ready, if someone handsome comes courting."

Athene knew that would get Nausicaa hurrying down to the river. And the washing pools were right by the place where Odysseus was hiding. Smiling to herself, the goddess flew back to high Olympus.

As rosy-fingered Dawn lit up the sky, Nausicaa awoke — and remembered her dream. Quickly she dressed and went to find her father.

"Please lend me a wagon," she said to King Alcinous, "to go down to the washing pools. I want to wash all my fine clothes — and yours, too. Just in case someone important comes calling."

She was too shy to mention what kind of "someone" she meant, but her father understood. Without asking questions, he told his men to prepare a mule cart.

Nausicaa went all around the palace, collecting armfuls of beautiful, brightly colored clothes. She packed them into the cart, and her mother filled a box with food and wine.

"Enjoy yourselves," she said.

Chattering and laughing, Nausicaa and her friends went down

to the washing pools. They had no idea that Odysseus was sleeping underneath the olive tree there. They expected to spend the whole day on their own.

At first they worked hard, treading the washing clean in the clear water. When that was done, they spread the clothes out to dry on the shingle while they bathed and enjoyed their picnic. Then Nausicaa sang to keep time while they played with a ball.

The clothes were dry and the girls were about to pack up and go home when Nausicaa threw the ball for the last time. One of her friends reached out to catch it — and missed. It slipped into the river, and they all shrieked loudly.

The noise awoke Odysseus.

He opened his eyes and sat up, instantly alert. Who were the people he could hear down by the river? Were they friendly or hostile? Human beings or gods? He was in no state to meet strangers, but he had to find out. He crawled out of his hiding place, breaking off a leafy branch to hide his nakedness, and, holding it in front of him, he walked down to the river.

He was a terrifying sight. His filthy skin was covered in scratches, his eyes were wild and desperate, and his whole body was crusted with salt. When the girls saw him, they screamed and ran away in all directions.

Only Nausicaa stood her ground. While the others hid in the bushes, she faced Odysseus, waiting for him to speak.

"Princess," he said, "I see that you're brave and beautiful. If you are human, too, have pity on me. I have been adrift for nineteen days on the dark sea. Yesterday I struggled ashore, but as you see, I have lost everything. Please give me some rags to cover my body, and tell me how to reach the nearest town."

"Sir," said Nausicaa, "I am the daughter of Alcinous, the king of this country. Since the gods have brought you here, of course we'll help you. My friends and I will give you some clothes. And when you have washed, we'll take you to the town."

She called to her maids, and they crept out of their hiding places. They chose a tunic and a cloak for Odysseus and gave him olive oil for his bath. Then they left him on his own to wash in the river.

When he came to find them again, he looked like a different person. He was clean from head to toe, and his newly washed hair hung in a thick, shining mass. Dressed in the bright cloak and tunic, he was the handsomest man Nausicaa had ever seen.

124

"That's the kind of husband I'd like," she whispered to her maids.

Wisely, she decided not to take him straight back to the palace. People were sure to gossip if she turned up with such a handsome stranger. Instead, she asked him to wait in a little wood just outside the town.

"Give us time to reach home," she said. "Then come after us. The palace is easy to find. Walk straight in and speak to my mother, Arete. She'll be sitting by the fireside, spinning purple yarn. Fling yourself at her feet and ask for help. If you win her over, she'll make sure you get home safely."

Leaving Odysseus in the wood, Nausicaa drove the cart back to the palace. As soon as he was alone, Odysseus sent up a prayer to Athene.

"May the Phaeacians treat me kindly," he said.

There was no immediate answer, but as he walked toward the town, Athene herself came to meet him, disguised as a young girl carrying a jar of water.

"Can you tell me the way to the palace?" Odysseus asked.

"I'll take you," said Athene. "But don't say a word to anyone on the way. The people here don't like strangers."

She wrapped him in a magic mist that made him invisible to everyone they passed. Then she led him along the quays and past the bustling harbors to the doors of King Alcinous's palace.

"Go straight inside," she said. "Don't speak until you reach Queen Arete. She is wise and noble, and if you touch her heart, you will have a good chance of reaching home at last."

Athene left him at the entrance to the palace. For a moment Odysseus stood still, staring up at the massive golden doors on their posts of silver. Then he stepped through, into the great hall.

The whole palace was bustling with activity, but Odysseus was still invisible. He walked straight past everything until he reached Queen Arete, spinning beside the hearth. As he flung himself down at her feet, the magic mist cleared suddenly, so that he seemed to appear out of nowhere.

There was a startled silence in the hall. Everyone stared at him.

He looked up at the queen and spoke in a clear voice. "Noble Arete, may the gods bless you and your family. I have suffered many hardships and disasters, and I need your help to reach my home again."

Bowing politely, he sat down in the ashes by the hearth to wait for the queen's reply. For a moment, no one knew what to say. Then a wise old lord called Echeneus broke the silence.

"King Alcinous," he said, "you don't usually leave your guests sitting in the ashes. Aren't you going to welcome this man?"

Immediately the king called for water to rinse Odysseus's hands and told the maids to bring him food and wine. "Refresh yourself, sir," he said. "Sleep in my palace tonight. Tomorrow I will ask you about your adventures, and then we can discuss your journey home."

Queen Arete ordered her maids to prepare a bed for Odysseus. That night he lay down under bright rugs and warm purple blankets, and slept soundly until morning.

The next day, King Alcinous gave orders for a ship to be made ready, with fifty-two young men to take the oars.

"This is for you, stranger," he said to Odysseus. "But before you leave, let us show you our Phaeacian hospitality."

He organized a great feast for Odysseus and invited the whole town. When everyone had eaten, the blind poet, Demodocus, took up his lyre and began to sing a story of the Trojan War.

Odysseus was cut to the heart, remembering his friends who had died in that war. King Alcinous saw his sad face, but he didn't ask any questions. Instead, as soon as the story was finished, he stood up and stepped back from the table.

"You have shared our feast," he said to Odysseus, "and heard our great poet sing. Now come and see how good our sportsmen are."

They flocked out of the palace, and all the young men started jumping and running. They set up wrestling matches and competed at throwing the discus. Everyone took part, including Prince Laodamas, Nausicaa's brother.

"And how about you, sir?" he said to Odysseus. "Would you like to share our sports?"

Odysseus shook his head. "Not after all I've been through. I need my strength for traveling home."

One of the other young men looked him up and down rudely. "You don't look much like an athlete," he said.

Odysseus was annoyed. "I used to be one of the best," he said sharply. "Let me show you what I can do, even now."

He jumped to his feet and seized the biggest, heaviest discus. Swinging his arm back, he flung it with all his strength — making the Phaeacians duck as it went flying over their heads.

It was a huge throw, beating all the other attempts. Odysseus watched it land and then turned to face his hosts.

"Is that enough?" he said. "Would you like me to throw again? Or does one of you want to challenge me to a boxing match? I can wrestle and run, too. And I am a better archer than anyone else on earth. How else would you like to test me?"

"Noble guest," said King Alcinous, "you have proved yourself already. I don't know who you are, but you're just the kind of man I'd like my daughter to marry."

Odysseus shook his head, smiling. "She is a beautiful, wise girl, but I have a wife already. And a son, too. I must go home to them."

"We'll send you on your way very soon," said Alcinous. "But first there are gifts we want to give you."

He led Odysseus back into the palace and presented him with a bronze and silver sword. The Phaeacian lords added so many other treasures that Alcinous had to provide a great wooden coffer to hold them all. Then they enjoyed a second feast together.

Afterward, Demodocus took up his lyre again. This time, he began to sing about the wooden horse that the Greeks had used to capture Troy.

"*Crafty Odysseus devised the plan,*
And built a hollow horse made out of wood.
The Greeks embarked, pretending to retreat
And left the horse behind upon the shore.
Triumphantly, the Trojans took it in,
Not guessing how they were deceived,
Not knowing Odysseus and his men
Were crouched inside. . . ."

Listening to the song, Odysseus saw the shadowy faces of his comrades, crouching beside him in the horse's belly.

He remembered those same faces lit with the fire of battle as they broke out of the horse and rampaged through the sleeping streets of Troy. Quietly he began to weep.

Alcinous signaled to the poet to stop singing. "Sir," he said to Odysseus, "we can see that you are noble, but you have not told us anything about yourself. Who are you? And why does this song cause you such grief?"

Odysseus drew a long breath. "I am Odysseus, Laertes's son," he said. "I was one of the men who crouched inside that wooden horse. I saw Troy fall and the whole city burn. And ever since then, I have been trying to get home to Ithaca."

Alcinous stared at him. "But it's almost ten years since the end of the Trojan War. Why has the journey taken you so long?"

Odysseus drew another breath. And then he began to tell the whole story of his travels, right from the beginning.

MEANWHILE, IN SPARTA, Telemachus was also listening to stories about his father's adventures.

"Odysseus is so clever!" Queen Helen said. "Once he disguised himself as a slave, in filthy rags, and sneaked into Troy to find out the Trojans' secrets."

"If he was so clever, why couldn't he save himself?" said Telemachus miserably. "He's dead — and our house is full of vile men who want to marry my mother."

"He's not dead!" said King Menelaus. "I know that for certain."

Telemachus caught his breath. "Tell me," he said. "*How* do you know?"

"When I was sailing back from Troy," said Menelaus, "my ships were becalmed in Egypt for twenty days. They would still be there if I hadn't been helped by a nymph — the daughter of the Old Man of the Sea. She took pity on us.

"'My father knows how you can get home,' she said. 'But he won't tell you unless you catch him. And you can only do that in the evening, when he comes out of the water to tend his seals. You must hide on the beach and seize him while he's counting them. Then you must hold him tightly until he stops changing his shape.'"

"How can anyone hide on a beach?" Telemachus said.

Menelaus smiled ruefully. "There was only one way. Four of us disguised ourselves in sealskins and lay on the beach with all the other seals. The stench was dreadful — but the plan worked. When the Old Man came to count his seals, we grabbed him and held him fast while he struggled to escape.

"He changed into a lion and then a snake. After that, he became a panther, then a giant bear. But the four of us clung on tightly through it all — even when he transformed himself into running water.

"Finally, he was too exhausted to change anymore. He returned to his own shape and told us how to reach home. And I asked him about all my comrades from Troy."

"Even my father?" said Telemachus.

Menelaus nodded. "I asked if he was dead. 'Not dead,' said the Old Man, 'but trapped on Calypso's island, with no ship to take him home.'"

"Where is that island?" Telemachus asked eagerly.

Menelaus shrugged. "Only the gods know where," he said.

BACK IN ALCINOUS'S PALACE, Odysseus came to the end of his story. When he stopped speaking, there was silence in the great hall.

"You have been through great suffering," Alcinous said at last. "But your journey is almost over. A ship is ready for you. At sunset, it will leave for Ithaca."

When the sun sank below the horizon, Odysseus thanked Alcinous and Arete for their help. Nausicaa came down to the harbor to say good-bye.

"Good luck go with you, my friend," she said. "Do not forget me when you come to your own country."

"How could I forget you?" Odysseus said. "You gave me back my life. If I reach Ithaca, I will think of you every single day."

As the stars began to come out, he boarded the ship, taking all the treasures the Phaeacians had given him. The oarsmen spread rugs in the stern so that he could sleep while they were traveling.

All through the night, the ship sped over the ocean like a falcon. When the morning star rose, it was close to Ithaca and Odysseus was still sleeping soundly.

The sailors didn't wake him. They lifted him carefully and took him ashore, laying him down on a sandy beach. His treasures were heaped up in the shade of an olive tree, where they would be safe until he awoke. He was still fast asleep when the ship set off back to Phaeacia.

BUT POSEIDON WASN'T sleeping. He was filled with a black and terrible rage when he saw Odysseus arriving back in Ithaca with more treasure than ever before.

"What mockery is this?" he bellowed at Zeus. "I left this vile man wrecked and destitute — and the Phaeacians have made him rich. I shall destroy their ship and drown the sailors! And I'll fling up a circle of huge mountains around their city to cut it off from the rest of the world. Let them learn to fear me!"

"Peace, earth shaker," said Zeus. "There is no need to ruin the city. If you must destroy the ship, simply turn it into a rock as it reaches the harbor. All the Phaeacians will see — and fear you forever."

The idea delighted Poseidon. He swooped toward the Phaeacians' city. As everyone onshore watched the ship approach, he struck at it with his hand, turning it to stone. Immediately, it stopped, rooted to the bottom of the sea.

The watchers on the shore didn't realize what had happened. Only King Alcinous understood.

"We have angered Poseidon," he said. "This Odysseus whom we helped is under his curse. We can't save him from that, but we can pray for Poseidon's forgiveness on our city."

They made a great sacrifice of bulls to Poseidon, and he relented and made peace with them. But every time they saw the stone ship outside the harbor, they pitied Odysseus for having such a powerful god as his enemy.

ODYSSEUS ᵀ BEGGAR

BUT ODYSSEUS HAD A POWERFUL FRIEND
as well. Athene was determined to help him back
to his rightful place. When she saw him asleep on
the beach in Ithaca, she knew he was in danger. If
the suitors found him on his own, they were sure
to kill him. She had to keep him away from the
palace until he figured out how to defeat them.

As a start, she covered the beach with a magic mist.
When Odysseus woke up, he didn't recognize the place.
He thought the Phaeacians had tricked him and taken
him somewhere else.

"They've stranded me in a strange country," he muttered
angrily. "And stolen all my treasure."

But then he looked around and saw the treasure, heaped up
under an olive tree. So what had happened? Where was he?

He was still wondering, when Athene came sauntering onto the beach, disguised as a shepherd boy. She greeted him cheerfully.

"Who are you?" she said. "What are you doing here?"

Odysseus had no idea who this shepherd boy was. So he lied about his name and started telling a false story.

Athene threw back her head and laughed. "Don't you know me? Don't you recognize your own land of Ithaca?"

Waving her hand, she lifted the mist and Odysseus realized who she was. He fell to his knees with a cry of joy. "Goddess, you have always been kind to me!"

"Now you need my help again," Athene said. "Your palace is full of men who want to marry your wife and kill your son. If you go there on your own, they will kill you, too."

"What should I do?" asked Odysseus.

"Go and find Eumaeus, your swineherd," Athene said. "He will let you stay in his hut until I bring Telemachus to you. But it's best if Eumaeus doesn't know who you are." She reached out her stick and touched Odysseus on the shoulder.

Immediately, his smooth skin creased into wrinkles. His thick, curly hair grew thin and straggling and turned gray. The fine clothes King Alcinous had given him were transformed into a beggar's rags.

Athene handed him a shabby knapsack and a rough wooden staff. "Off to the swineherd's hut," she said. "Wait there for Telemachus. He is away on a voyage, but I will fetch him home."

As she sped off, Odysseus hid his treasure. Then he trudged up the rough track to Eumaeus's hut. The swineherd was sitting outside with his dogs. When they saw Odysseus, they flew at him, barking wildly, and they would have attacked him if Eumaeus hadn't called them off.

"You're lucky I was here," he said. "Come into my hut and recover, old man."

He gave Odysseus bread to eat while he prepared a meal.

"It won't be much," he said ruefully. "All the best pigs go to those greedy suitors in the palace. Now that my master's dead and gone, they spend the whole day feasting there, and guzzling his wine."

"Is your master really dead?" Odysseus said carefully. "Who was he?"

"He's probably a skeleton by now." Eumaeus shook his head sadly. "He went off to the war in Troy twenty years ago, and he never came back. Oh, my noble master! How I miss him."

"Tell me his name," Odysseus said. "I fought in that war too. I might be able to give you some news."

"I know that kind of *news,*" Eumaeus said bitterly. "Every beggar who comes here has some tale to tell Penelope, my mistress. She's so desperate for news of her husband that she listens to them all. And then she showers them with gifts — which is what they were after, of course. I'd like to hear the story of your adventures, stranger — but no lies about Odysseus."

Odysseus found it hard not to say who he was, but he obeyed Athene's instructions. He invented a story about travels in Egypt, and then Eumaeus made him up a bed beside the fire.

So Odysseus spent his first night back in Ithaca in a swineherd's hut, with Eumaeus's old cloak over him to keep out the cold.

MEANWHILE, ATHENE was speeding toward
Sparta to bring Telemachus home. When she arrived there,
she appeared to him in a vision.

"Why are you still in Sparta, Telemachus?" she said. "You've
left your mother unguarded—and your treasures, too. And
now those evil suitors are plotting to kill you. They're going to
ambush your ship as you sail past the island of Asteris."

"How can I escape?" said Telemachus.

"Don't anchor at Asteris for the night," Athene told him.
"Travel on through the dark until you reach Ithaca. But don't
stay on your ship while it sails into the harbor. Get your sailors
to drop you off before that, at the first headland. Then go
straight to Eumaeus's hut. You can trust him."

Telemachus was wide awake now — and anxious to go home. As soon as it was morning, he said good-bye to Menelaus and Helen and they sent him on his way with many treasures.

He was about to leave when a great eagle came flying across the sky carrying a fat goose from someone's farmyard.

"That's a sign from the gods!" cried Helen joyfully. "As that eagle came down from the mountains and pounced on the fat goose, so Odysseus will return and swoop down on the wicked suitors who are fattening themselves in your palace."

"May that be true!" Telemachus said fervently. He said farewell and set off as fast as he could, ordering his ship to put to sea immediately.

Athene gave them a following wind, and they sailed steadily until sunset. As night fell, the island of Asteris came into view, and the sailors looked at Telemachus, expecting orders to land.

But Telemachus had not forgotten Athene's warning. "We sail on," he told the sailors. "There's no time to rest." Obediently they kept a straight course, and Telemachus stared into the darkness, wondering what fate was in store for him. Would he reach home alive, or would he be caught by the evil suitors?

EARLY THE NEXT MORNING, when Odysseus and Eumaeus were preparing their breakfast in the hut, the dogs began to bark loudly.

"There's someone coming," Odysseus said.

Eumaeus went to the door and gave a cry of joy. "Telemachus, light of my eyes, you're safe! Come in."

Walking into the hut, Telemachus saw the ragged beggar inside. "Greetings, stranger," he said politely.

"Our visitor's a real traveler," Eumaeus said. "I've done my best to entertain him, but now that you're home, you can give him a proper welcome."

"How can I invite him to my house?" Telemachus said ruefully. "Think how those wicked suitors will insult him." He sat down on a heap of branches next to Odysseus. "Good Eumaeus, please go and tell my mother that I'm home. But make sure no one else hears you."

"Trust me," Eumaeus said. Putting on his sandals, he set off straightaway.

As soon as he was out of sight, Athene came to the door of the hut, in the shape of a tall and beautiful woman. She stood out of sight of Telemachus, where only Odysseus and the dogs could see her.

The dogs whimpered and ran off to the far side of the farmyard. Glancing up, Odysseus met Athene's eyes and knew at once who she was. Muttering an excuse to Telemachus, he stood up and slipped out of the hut.

Athene led him away from the door. "Noble Odysseus," she said, "the time has come to tell Telemachus everything. Then the two of you must decide how to get rid of these wicked suitors who are ruining Ithaca. Go back inside and greet your son."

She waved her staff. Immediately Odysseus's disguise was stripped away. His body straightened, his hair and beard were thick and dark again, and his wrinkles disappeared. The beggar's stinking rags were replaced by fresh, clean clothes.

When he stepped back into the hut, Telemachus looked up and gasped.

"Stranger, who are you?" he said in an awed voice. "Only the gods can change like that. Have mercy on me."

"I am no god," said Odysseus. "I'm your father, Telemachus."

Telemachus stared — and then flung his arms around Odysseus's neck in tears of joy. Quickly, Odysseus gave an account of his adventures and how he'd come to be in Eumaeus's hut.

". . . and now there's work to do," he finished. "You and I must get rid of these suitors who are devouring our island."

"If only we could!" Telemachus said. "I know you are a great warrior, Father, but there are over a hundred suitors. How can we fight so many men on our own?"

"We're not on our own," said Odysseus. "Athene is on our side, and so is Zeus himself, the father of gods and men. Isn't that enough help for you?"

"The gods are powerful allies," said Telemachus. "But I still don't see how two men can defeat a hundred enemies."

"That's what we're going to figure out now," Odysseus said. "Listen. . . ."

Lowering his voice, he began to explain his plan.

Down in the town, Eumaeus took his message to Penelope, but there was no hope of keeping it secret. The returning sailors were already spreading the news.

"Telemachus is alive!" they shouted as they came up from the harbor.

The suitors were furious — and so was Penelope. As soon as Eumaeus had gone, she swept down from her room in a rage.

"What kind of men are you?" she said to the suitors. "You're all guests here, living at Odysseus's expense — and now you've tried to kill his son!"

The suitors swore it wasn't true. "All we want is for you to choose another husband," they said. "But you keep putting us off. First you wouldn't choose until Telemachus was a man. And now you're pretending to weave a shroud."

"I *am* weaving!" Penelope said fiercely.

But one of her maids had betrayed her. "Every night you unpick your weaving!" said an angry suitor. "We know what you're doing, Penelope. You can't delay any longer. It's time to choose."

They all clamored at her, until she went back up to her room in tears. Much as she loathed the idea, she had to do what they demanded. She couldn't see any escape from the situation.

She didn't know that Odysseus and Telemachus were in the swineherd's hut at that very moment, plotting how to rescue her.

By the time Eumaeus returned to the hut, Athene had changed Odysseus back into an old beggar. And the old beggar insisted that he wanted to visit the palace in the morning.

Telemachus pretended to be impatient with him. "Well, I'm much too busy to take you in. You'll have to wait until Eumaeus is ready."

"That suits me fine," croaked Odysseus. "I'd rather wait till it warms up a little. These frosty mornings are no good for my old bones."

So first thing in the morning, Telemachus set off to the palace on his own, leaving the other two to trail along behind. King Odysseus went back to his palace dressed in rags and leaning on a stick. He looked so old and dirty that the goatherd shouted abuse at him as he came past with the goats.

"What are you doing, you greasy old plate-licker? Are you heading into town to grovel around for scraps? Why don't you try a bit of honest work?"

Odysseus was itching to give him a crack on the head with his stick, but that would have ruined his plan. He put up patiently with the insults, hobbling on down the path until he and Eumaeus came in sight of the palace.

"You go in first," Odysseus said. "I'll follow behind you."

As he spoke, there was a movement on the far side of the courtyard, over by the dung heap. Catching the sound of Odysseus's voice, an old, old dog lifted his head and began to wag his tail. But he couldn't get up and walk toward them. He was too weak to move.

When Odysseus saw the dog, his eyes filled with tears. "What's a lovely dog like that doing on the dung heap?" he muttered.

"Ah, that's Argus, Odysseus's old dog," Eumaeus said. "He used to be a marvelous hunting dog, but the heart went out of him when Odysseus sailed away."

He walked off into the palace, and the old dog lowered his head and slumped back onto the dung heap. Odysseus hurried toward him, but he was too late. The light faded from the old dog's eyes before Odysseus could reach him. He had managed to hang on just long enough to see his master again, but now he was dead.

Sadly Odysseus walked into the great hall of the palace. The suitors were feasting and listening to music, and he began to go from table to table, begging for scraps of food. Some of the suitors gave him bread and meat from their plates, but some of them just insulted him.

"We've got enough beggars around already," said one.

"Can't you spare me a little piece of bread?" Odysseus said. "After all, you're getting it free."

The suitor was outraged. He picked up a wooden stool and threw it hard, hitting Odysseus in the back. A weaker man would have been knocked off his feet. Odysseus stayed steady — but that was only the first attack.

Another beggar appeared in the hall doorway, a greedy hulk of a man called Irus. He was furious to see a rival beggar in the hall, and he charged at Odysseus, intending to throw him out.

"A fight, a fight!" the suitors shouted in delight. "Let's see who's the best wrestler!"

They jumped up and crowded around, egging Irus on and cheering drunkenly as Odysseus tucked up his rags. Odysseus knew he could win easily, but he chose not to hurt Irus too much. He beat him just enough to make his nose bleed — which raised a cheer from the suitors — and then dumped him outside the hall.

At that moment, Penelope appeared, coming slowly down the stairs. She looked so beautiful that all the suitors stopped shouting and fell silent, feeling as though their bones were melting. Each of them remembered, all over again, why he was there, and how much he wanted to marry her.

Penelope went over to Telemachus. "You shouldn't let them treat your guest like that," she whispered, pointing to Odysseus.

"How can I control the suitors?" Telemachus muttered.

Penelope was still watching Odysseus. "He may be only a beggar," she murmured, "but he's under our protection. And maybe he has news about your father. I'll speak with him this evening, when the suitors have gone."

Telemachus went over to tell Odysseus and the suitors came crowding around Penelope, paying her compliments and competing for her attention. With a sigh, she turned to face them.

"Don't waste your breath on flattery," she said. "The only praise I valued was from Odysseus. But I can see those days are over. All I can do now is obey his wishes."

The suitors stopped talking, wondering what she was going to say.

Penelope sighed again. "Before Odysseus went away to Troy, he warned me that he might be killed. He said that if he didn't come back, I should marry again when Telemachus was a man."

Now the hall was completely silent. Penelope drew a long breath, steadying her voice.

"The time has come," she said. "Tomorrow, I shall do as Odysseus wanted, and choose a new husband."

The suitors were jubilant. As Penelope walked back upstairs, they went home for the night, celebrating drunkenly. Tomorrow, one of them would be Penelope's new husband.

That was what they thought. But Odysseus had other plans.

As soon as all the suitors had gone, he and Telemachus moved around the hall by torchlight. They cleared away all the armor and weapons that were stacked against the walls and locked them in the storeroom. Tomorrow, there would be no weapons in the hall except their own.

When every last sword and helmet was gone, Telemachus went off to his own room for the night and Odysseus settled down beside the fire. As soon as he was on his own, Penelope came down from her room again, accompanied by Eurycleia, the old nurse.

"Sit here with me," she said to Odysseus, "and tell me about your voyages. Have you heard news of my husband on your travels?"

Odysseus longed to tell her who he was. But he had to get rid of the suitors first. So, to comfort her, he made up a tale about meeting Odysseus in Crete.

"And he's on his way home now," he finished. "Before the month is over, he will be here with you. I swear it."

"If only I could believe that." Penelope sighed. "But I've promised to choose a new husband tomorrow. I'm going to challenge the suitors to string Odysseus's great bow. If one of them can do that, and shoot an arrow through the loops of ten bronze axes, he will be my next husband."

Her idea fitted in perfectly with Odysseus's plan. He nodded approvingly. "Keep to what you've decided," he said. "Before the contest is over, Odysseus will be here to rescue you."

Penelope shook her head and stood up. "We shall see," she said sadly. "Meanwhile, you are welcome in my palace. Eurycleia will bring you some water so that you can wash."

She went back to her room, and Eurycleia came bustling over with a bowl of water. Kneeling down, she began to wash Odysseus's dusty feet. As she dried them, her fingers touched an old scar on his leg.

Her hands stopped moving, and she froze for a moment. Then, with trembling fingers, she parted his rags to look at the scar. It was a long, pale ridge, where an old wound had healed.

"You got that in a boar hunt," she whispered. "When you were just a boy." Slowly she looked up at his face. "Oh, my dear master," she said.

"Hush!" Odysseus put a finger to his lips. "Keep my secret, if you want me to drive out those wicked suitors."

"I will!" Eurycleia said grimly. "They've corrupted the maids and almost ruined this island. They all deserve to be punished."

"Tomorrow they will be," said Odysseus.

Then he settled down beside the hearth, staring into the fire and waiting for morning to come.

A HUSBAND FOR PENELOPE

||||||||||||||||||||||||||||||||||||||||||||

As a rosy Dawn crept across the sky,
Penelope was down in the storeroom, fetching
Odysseus's great bow. She picked it up, with
its long string hanging loose, and found
a quiver full of arrows. Then she ordered
Eurycleia to bring up all the bronze and iron
axes that Odysseus had won as trophies.

By the time the suitors arrived, everything was ready
for the contest. Telemachus had set up the axes in a line
down the center of the hall, and Penelope was sitting
by the hearth with the great bow in her hand.

"This is how I shall choose my next husband," she announced.
"I shall marry the man who can string this bow and use it to
shoot an arrow through the loops of all these axes."

"I must attempt it too," Telemachus said. "No one shall touch
my father's bow before I have tried my strength and skill."

A CONTEST OF STRENGTH AND SKILL

He picked up the bow in both hands. Three times he tried to bend it, but he couldn't quite loop the string into place.

At his fourth attempt he might have managed it, but Odysseus warned him off with a tiny shake of his head. That wouldn't fit their plan.

As soon as Telemachus put down the bow, the suitors came crowding forward, each determined to pass the test and win Penelope. One by one, they picked up the bow and struggled to string it, but no one was strong enough.

While they were struggling, Odysseus stepped outside the hall and went to find Eumaeus.

"Faithful friend," he said. "It's time to tell you who I am."

He parted his rags to show the long, silvery scar on his leg. When Eumaeus saw it, his face lit up and he opened his mouth to shout for joy.

"Stay quiet!" hissed Odysseus. "First we must drive out these wicked men. Go around the hall and lock all the other doors so that no one can escape."

"It will be a pleasure!" Eumaeus said fiercely. "And when I've done that, I'll come back to fight with you — and I'll bring the cowherd with me. You still have a few loyal servants here."

He set off at once, and Odysseus slipped back into the hall to watch the next man wrestling with his bow.

There were more than a hundred of them, and the contest lasted all day. One suitor after another came forward, eager to take his turn. One by one they failed, abandoning their hopes and passing the bow on to the next man.

Finally, as the sun began to set, the last suitor laid the bow aside, and a hush fell over the hall. Odysseus stepped forward.

"Lady," he said to Penelope, "may I try the bow?"

The suitors were outraged. They began to shout at him, but Penelope waved them aside.

"Yes, you may try," she said. "If you succeed, I won't marry you, but you will have a rich reward."

Telemachus pretended to be outraged too. "You'd let a beggar touch my father's bow? Go to bed, mother. This is a matter for men."

Penelope bowed her head and left them, and Odysseus picked up his bow. Ignoring the jeers of the suitors, he ran his hands over the wood. When he was sure it was sound, he bent the bow easily and slipped the string into its place.

A silence fell over the hall.

Odysseus plucked the bowstring, and it gave out a note as clear as a swallow's song. Then he took an arrow and set it on the string, taking aim at the axes. Moving so that all the rings were in line, he drew the arrow back and paused for a second. Then he let it go.

The arrow sped straight and true, flying through every one of the ax rings. It buried itself in the wall at the far end of the hall, and Odysseus turned to Telemachus.

"I have not disgraced you, my son," he said. "Now let's give the suitors their supper — and see them dance."

"Yes, Father!" said Telemachus.

With horror, the suitors realized who the beggar really was. Odysseus moved into the main doorway, and Telemachus sprang to his side, sword and spear in hand. Eumaeus and the cowherd stepped up behind them, and Odysseus took another arrow from his quiver.

The suitors began to panic — especially when they discovered that all the other doors were locked.

"We'll pay for every mouthful we've eaten," they babbled. "We'll give you piles of gold and herds of oxen — if you'll only let us go."

"Gold and oxen can't pay for what you've done!" Odysseus said fiercely. "What I want is justice! You've dishonored my house and almost ruined Ithaca with your greed. Stand up and fight!"

There were over a hundred suitors and only four men in the doorway, but the suitors knew Odysseus's reputation. Their hands trembled as they drew their swords.

And then the battle began. . . .

It was a bloody and terrifying fight. Odysseus allowed a few of the men to escape with their lives, but the others had to pay for their crimes. By the time the battle was over, almost all the suitors were dead.

Odysseus gave orders for the bodies to be removed. Then he had the hall cleaned, and purified it with fire and sulfur. When everything was as it used to be, he sent Eurycleia upstairs to announce that he was home.

The old nurse ran to Penelope's room and leaned over her bed.

"Wake up!" she said. "Your prayers have all been answered. Odysseus is here!"

Penelope lifted her head from the pillow. "Don't make fun of me," she said.

"I'm serious," Eurycleia insisted. "That old beggar was Odysseus in disguise. And now he's destroyed all your wicked suitors. Come and see."

Penelope still didn't believe her. "How could one man on his own defeat so many people? If the suitors have really been killed, it must have been done by one of the gods. Odysseus died long ago, in some far-off foreign land."

"What nonsense!" Eurycleia said. "Come downstairs and you'll see."

"I'll come to see Telemachus," Penelope replied, "but I won't let a trickster take me in."

She got out of bed and walked to the top of the stairs. Looking down, she saw the great hall, empty and clean at last, with the fresh wind blowing through it. And there in the middle of the hall was Telemachus, standing shoulder to shoulder with the ragged beggar.

Could that really be Odysseus? Penelope was afraid to believe it. She had been fooled too many times before and heard too many lies. Ignoring the beggar completely, she went straight to Telemachus and hugged him.

"What's the matter with you?" said Telemachus. "Can't you see my father here? You've waited so long. Why don't you greet him now?"

Penelope looked sideways at the beggar. "If he really is my husband," she said, "I shall know soon enough. Odysseus and I share many secrets that no one else knows."

Telemachus shook his head impatiently, but Odysseus stayed calm. He had waited a long time already, but he was wise and patient.

"Give your mother a chance to make up her mind," he said to Telemachus. "Let's bathe and put on clean clothes. Then we'll ask the musicians to play some dancing music — and see what happens."

The two of them went away to wash off the blood from the fight. Then Odysseus dressed in his own royal clothes and went out into the hall.

Penelope was sitting beside the fire, staring into the flames and listening to the music. Quietly, Odysseus sat down next to her.

"What an odd woman you are," he murmured. "Here I am, back after twenty years, and you won't even speak to me. Any other woman would have thrown herself into her husband's arms." He raised his voice and called out to Eurycleia. "Find me a bed of my own. I can't sleep with my wife. Her heart is as hard as iron."

"What an odd man you are," Penelope replied. "I'm not hard-hearted — just careful. I've been faithful to Odysseus for twenty years, and I'm not going to let an impostor deceive me. You don't look like the man who sailed away twenty years ago." She turned around and nodded at Eurycleia. "Do as our visitor asks. Move the great bed out of my husband's and my old bedroom and make it up for him down here."

As she gave the order, she was watching the man beside her. Only she and Odysseus knew the secret of that bed. If this stranger stayed silent now, he was certainly *not* her husband.

But he didn't stay silent. As soon as she finished speaking, Odysseus jumped up, roaring with anger.

"Woman, what have you done? I built that bed around an ancient olive tree. The first bedpost was made from the tree trunk — still rooted in the ground. Have you let someone cut through that trunk and move our bed?"

Penelope started trembling with joy. She burst into tears and threw her arms around Odysseus.

"It's you!" she said. "Oh, Odysseus, it's really you! Don't be angry with me. No one has cut through the bedpost. But I've always been afraid that someone would come here and trick me by pretending to be you. So I thought up this plan to make sure I couldn't be deceived. Because no one knows the secret of the bed except you and me."

Odysseus hugged her hard, almost in tears himself. "How faithful and true you are," he said. "How wise and beautiful. I am a happy man to come home to such a wife."

"Promise me that you'll never leave again," Penelope said.

Odysseus hesitated.

"What's the matter?" said Penelope quickly.

Odysseus was remembering the prophecy of blind old Tiresias, down in the Land of the Dead.

If you want to be free of Poseidon's curse, you must make another journey. Travel inland with an oar over your shoulder, until you are far away from the sea. When someone mistakes your oar for a winnowing fan, sacrifice to Poseidon there. Then he will let you live in peace again.

Slowly he repeated the words to Penelope. Her heart sank at the thought of losing him again. But she didn't waver.

"We can't live peacefully," she said, "while one of the gods is your enemy. If that is the price of a happy old age, then you must make that journey."

Odysseus hugged her again, knowing now that there would be a peaceful end to all his travels. Then he and Penelope walked up the stairs to their old room, beginning to tell each other the long story of all that had happened in the last twenty years.

G R E E K A L P H A B E T

ΕΛΛΗΝΙΚΟ ΑΛΦΑΒΗΤΟ

A a	B b	G g	D d	E e	Z z
alpha	beta	gamma	delta	epsilon	zeta
άλφα	βήτα	γάμμα	δέλτα	έψιλον	ζήτα

E e	TH th	I i	K k	L l	M m
eta	theta	iota	κάρρα	lambda	mu
ήτα	θήτα	ιώτα	καππα	λάμδα	μυ

N n	KS ks	O o	P p	R r	S s
nu	xi	omicron	pi	rho	sigma
νυ	ξι	όμικρον	πι	ρω	σίγμα

T t	U u	PH ph	CH ch	PS ps	O o
tau	upsilon	phi	chi	psi	omega
ταυ	ύψιλον	φι	χι	ψι	ωμέγα

THE MYSTERY OF
HOMER

The *Odyssey* is one of the greatest pieces
of storytelling in the world. And one of the oldest.
For almost three thousand years, people have read
about the adventures of Odysseus as he roamed
the wide sea after the Trojan War, struggling
to get home to the rocky island of Ithaca.
But what about the storyteller?
Who *was* Homer?
That's one of the great mysteries of literature.

According to ancient tradition, Homer was a blind poet. But maybe he was described like that simply because blind people were thought to have special insight, and the power to foresee the future.

Modern experts think he lived on the coast of Turkey in the eighth century BC — but the date and the place aren't certain.

And although we *think* his name was Homer, we can't be sure of that, either. Perhaps there was no such person.

What *do* we know?

It seems clear that Homer (whoever he was) didn't invent these tales of men and gods and monsters. They had been told for maybe five hundred years before he lived. Before history could be written down, songs and stories were the best way of commemorating the great deeds of kings and heroes. The stories may have changed over hundreds of years of telling, but somewhere behind all the fantastic details of squabbling gods and terrifying monsters, there may well be a core of truth about things that actually happened.

Poets sang or chanted these stories from memory, and because the songs were long and complicated, they used special tricks to help them remember.

So, for example, they used set phrases and descriptions over and over again, talking about "the wine-dark sea" or "the wily Odysseus."

Some of these set phrases have survived into the *Odyssey*, reminding us of its ancient oral roots. So if Homer didn't invent these stories, why is he famous? Why do we care who he was?

The answer lies in the *Odyssey* itself. It's not just a collection of linked tales. The stories are wound together so skillfully that they become a single narrative. And

there are three strands of suspense that run all the way through.

Will Telemachus dodge the suitors' ambush and get back home safely? Will Penelope manage to fend off the suitors until her husband returns? Will Odysseus get back to Ithaca and be reunited with his wife?

The Greeks of Homer's time were very different from us in many ways. Their attitude to religion seems strange to us, and so does their glorification of battles and fighting. But the way Homer presents Odysseus's adventures makes it easy to sympathize with him. He's a hero who still has a wide appeal today. When I told my friends I was working on a retelling of the *Odyssey*, the most unexpected people said, "I love the *Odyssey*! I've loved it all my life!"

And that's the real mystery, of course. That, thousands of years ago, a man whose name we can't be sure of could sit down at a time we don't know exactly, in a place we can only guess, and write something that still moves and excites us today.

Gillian Cross

The author, illustrator, and publishers

would like to thank Dr. Anna Collar for all her help

and advice in the making of this book.

Retelling copyright © 2012 by Gillian Cross
Illustrations copyright © 2012 by Neil Packer

First U.S. edition 2012

Library of Congress Cataloging-in-Publication Data is available.
Library of Congress Catalog Card Number 2012289014
ISBN 978-0-7636-4791-9

16 17 TLF 10 9 8

Printed in Dongguan, Guangdong, China

This book was typeset in Skia.
The illustrations were done in gouache, pen, and wash.

Candlewick Press
99 Dover Street
Somerville, Massachusetts 02144

visit us at www.candlewick.com